T2-CSE-672

Damage Noted

DATE DUE 7/02

AG 27 02			
NO 11 02			
JL 08 2008			
GAYLORD			PRINTED IN U.S.A.

Shotgun Law

Shotgun Law

Nelson Nye

Thorndike Press • Chivers Press
Waterville, Maine USA Bath, England

This Large Print edition is published by Thorndike Press, USA and by Chivers Press, England.

Published in 2002 in the U.S. by arrangement with Golden West Literary Agency.

Published in 2002 in the U.K. by arrangement with Golden West Literary Agency.

U.S. Hardcover 0-7862-4157-8 (Western Series)
U.K. Hardcover 0-7540-4977-9 (Chivers Large Print)
U.K. Softcover 0-7540-4978-7 (Camden Large Print)

The text of this Large Print edition is unabridged.
Other aspects of the book may vary from the original edition.

Cover design by Thorndike Press Staff.

Set in 16 pt. Plantin.

Printed in the United States on permanent paper.

British Library Cataloguing in Publication Data available

Library of Congress Cataloging-in-Publication Data

Nye, Nelson C. (Nelson Coral), 1907–
   [Tinbadge]
   Shotgun law / Nelson Nye.
     p. cm.
   ISBN 0-7862-4157-8 (lg. print : hc : alk. paper)
   1. Sheriffs — Fiction. 2. Kidnapping — Fiction. 3. Large type books. I. Title.

PS3527.Y33 T56 2002
813'.54—dc21
                                    2002020719

Shotgun Law

1

With a face gone white as wood-ash, Girt Sasabe stepped from the saddle a short ten paces from the gathered cowhands hugging precious shade beneath the warped plank awning of Broken Stirrup's general store. Deliberately he lifted the sleek-barreled .45 from its open-topped holster, inspected its mechanism with the judgment of long acquaintance and slipped it back in leather.

Straightening, he eyed Cash Benson with a cold eye.

Sudden silence enveloped the lounging punchers. Through it Sasabe's spurs cut a wicked sound as he approached the steps.

Cash Benson's stocky shoulders stirred a little as those about him eased away. But there was a pride about this Benson that would not be shoved aside. His hard blue jaw snapped forward and a sneer curled his thin lips fleetingly as Sasabe stopped before him.

He was tall and gaunt, this Sasabe; a yellow-haired buck with eyes blue as turquoise and a red, weathered neck that looked near choked by the grip of the scarf knotted round it. His half-boots meeched on run-over heels and the spurs he'd strapped aboard them were as sorry a pair of gut hooks as could be found in a hundred miles. He needed a haircut worse than a shave; and the shave so bad you'd have sworn he was fresh out of hiding. But he commanded men's thoughts and their eyes and their listeners. For this was Torrance County — second toughest in the Territory and — though he mightn't be twenty till grass — Girt Sasabe was its sheriff.

His drawl was cold as gun steel. "Reckon I'm gettin' in my dotage, Benson — I'd of swore I ordered you out."

A grin crooked Benson's mouth. "Got an option on this lan'scape?"

"You bet!" Sasabe tapped his gun-butt. "I ain't goin' to fool with you, Benson. I want you out of the county by sundown."

And still the half smile clung to Benson's lip. "Talk's cheap," he shrugged. "Takes hard cash to buy good likker."

Sasabe's gaze roved the watchers' faces. Someone scuffled a boot uneasily.

The sheriff's cold look snapped back to Benson. He said distinctly: "You've one

8

chance, Benson. This is it. Don't be around come sundown."

He was moving toward his horse, moving down the steps, when a man came from the store; with a scowl stopped beside Cash Benson. "Must think he's Gawd A'mighty!" The words were loud — deliberately so.

Sasabe stopped on the steps and turned. "Nobody asked for your ante, Valmora."

"You got it anyhow." Yorba Joe Valmora sneered. " 'F I was you, I'd be steppin' mighty easy if I set any store by my health."

Sasabe nodded. "I reckon you would — it's the Injun in you, Joe." He said sharply, bleakly: "You ain't scarin' nobody with a *bone* in his spinal column. When the stage pulls out you be on it with a ticket reading same as Benson's. Ought to go a long ways together, you two. An' the longer the way, the better the county'll be suited."

The breed's eyes went snaky; shone like bits of jet. He was fast — *damned* fast. The down-wheeling of his hand was just a blur.

But the sheriff's whole body blurred. His right fist struck the breed's locked jaw — the sound was like a bat colliding. Valmora's mouth went twisted. His eyes bugged out like knobs on a stick; and were still that way when Sasabe's left drove him crashing through the door. His spurs got tangled. The jarring of his fall was like the belt of heavy thunder.

Cash Benson's hand jumped hipward.

Sasabe's glance-edge caught the movement. He spun, grabbing Benson's flexing wrist as it rose gun-weighted; jerked it in a savage hammerlock. Benson's gun went across the porch.

Sasabe released the wrist, stood back watching Benson rub it.

Benson's grin licked a wicked line. "Slick! You win this, bucko. But there'll come a day —"

"Don't lean too heavy on it." Sasabe throttled his breath down till he got his words squeezed even. "When the stage goes out tonight, be on it — both of you; or this'll be the last day's air you'll poison."

He turned on his heel, started again for his horse.

"Look out!" screamed a girl's scared voice.

Sasabe jumped straight out from the creaking steps — whirled twice. He came down on his toes with a gun gripped and ready.

Cash Benson tried to check his lunge — too late! The momentum of it carried him into Sasabe's arms and they both went down in a cursing tangle; clawing, slugging, grunting. Dust bulged round them.

The sheriff came out of it crouched and ready, his blue eyes slit-slim, flashing. Benson came red-eyed after him, every breath an effort, almost choking in his rage. There was a knife gripped in his stretched right fist. Sasabe knocked it from him, cursing.

His left hand dipped — *Benson's.* Got hold of a gun again. "By Gawd," he snarled, "I'm —"

"You're goin' to shout, too!" Sasabe snapped. "Your kind will eat with a snake! Put down that gun or set it smokin'!"

They glared across three feet of stillness.

No one spoke. No one cleared his throat or moved a foot or anything.

With a blur of motion a girl thrust forward; shoved a hand at either chest. "Men — *please!*"

Darinthy-May Tolliver. The girl whose cry had saved Sasabe's life. Biscuit shooter — ran the Honky-Donk Hash House south of Plain Street. Kind of gangling-like she was, and bony, with a mop of carrot hair and freckles spattered across her face like fly specks on a bar clock. She still had her greasy apron on and Levis under it like a

11

man. Just about as strong as a man she was too — as Girt found out when she shoved him back.

A growl welled from Benson's throat.

"Get back!" said Sasabe, impatient. "Back to your pots an' pans, girl — this is *men's* work! Leave it be!"

"Indeed!" She laughed at him, scornful; planted herself there solidly like she never meant to move. "Men's work, is it? Well, I'm glad you told me — I thought it was a couple of fence cats!"

Her bright glance left the sear of a whip.

But it didn't sear Benson. He said: "Get back!" stiff-lipped. Said with eyes on Girt: "Get out of the way, D'rinthy!"

"Not on your tintype!" Darinthy-May flared. "Think I want my place shot up? — all my winders busted an' what not? G'on out on the range someplace if you're so frothin' to riddle each other. G'on up a draw where it won't cost the town no money!"

Some light-headed fool started laughing.

Girt Sasabe was young enough to feel his face get hot. How come this . . . this *Tolliver tomcat* always tried to make him look ridiculous? Why'd she want to anyway? What'd she got against him? Why, he'd never spoken ten words to the girl!

12

Benson reached to brush her aside. "Put your gun up, Cash," Girt said, "an' I'll sheath mine."

Benson sneered. "Where's all that sand your craw was full of? What's happened to that bone in your spinal column — did it *melt?*"

Sasabe glared. But he didn't say quite what the store-front loungers expected. He didn't say anything. Nor did he bat Cash Benson down.

It was just like out of the catalog, what he was looking at — a girl on a high-stepping palomino. The last word in everything proper! Girt was so taken up he never noticed Darinthy-May quit the crowd; nor the scorn she showed in doing so. All but that part of his glance caution bade him reserve to Benson, he was bestowing whole-heartedly on the vision in catalog toggery.

She was quite an eyeful, right enough. Smart as a buggy whip! She'd a touch of the sunrise in her cheeks and sparkly eyes and hair like gold bright-scraped from a miner's pick. She was the handsomest thing, Girt Sasabe thought, that had ever come down the pike.

It made his ears roar just to look at her; and his heart beat so fast he thought it

13

would bust plumb out of his ribs.

That funny little bonnet, now! Why, it was just like it had been made for her — made to frame her face and the bright gold curls about. And her profile — it was just like that cameo Benson wore on his middle finger!

Girt didn't like that much; it made him jealous. But when she stared up at him smiling, blushing prettily under his own stare, Girt forgot Cash Benson utterly.

But Benson had not forgot anything. A grin licked his lips; and a flick of the wrist tipped his gun so it covered the loungers. Yorba Joe, bloody-faced, was crouched in the doorframe; and Benson gave him the nod.

Heaps of merchandise cluttered the porch just the way the freight wagons had left it. Wheelbarrows, mining and farming implements — a raft of stuff for the taking.

Cat-quiet, the breed took a pick handle — swung it!

The gleaming hickory took Girt Sasabe hard across the shoulders; sprawled him groggy in the dust. Not even the girl's cry budged him — it was like he'd fallen on flypaper.

Then everything went black.

2

"How many times I got to tell yer? Golrammit! You want I should croshay it on a *sampler*? *Sure* they got her! Grabbed 'er up like a chunk of fire an' cut hellbent fo' the border!"

The words drummed through Girt Sasabe's daze. Sloshing water from his face, the sheriff opened his eyes to find a mob tight packed about him. In the foreground stood a guy with a dripping bucket and the looks on the faces nearest would hardly have proved encouraging to a salesman of Bible tracts. This did not look like a Bible tract gathering.

Sasabe clawed himself erect and, brushing aside those who sought to detain him, stumbled through the crowd to where the talk was coming from. It was Andy McFarron, the storekeeper, who was throwing his jaw around. Facing him, mouth clamped and cheeks gone savage, was a heavy, well dressed fellow whose hair, mustache and short chinbeard were black as jet, whose eyes plowed through a man like an X-ray and who was very plainly furious. "An' the bunch of you stood around and *watched* it?"

"Hell," said McFarron defensively, "we'd no call to interfere. The sheriff was layin' down the law to Cash an' —"

"The sheriff! Where is he?"

"Right here, Mister Matheson —"

"So! And what were *you* doing while my daughter was being kidnaped?" Bitterness and accusation rode the banker's tones, and Sasabe's cheeks took on a flush while the crowd looked on approvingly. It was grown considerably larger than it had been when he talked to Benson; and he thought, not without some rancor, that it felt brave as hell now Benson was no longer around.

He said: "These gents can tell you all that. Important thing now is to get on their trail." He grabbed at the nearest lounger and the grip of him made the man wince. "Which way did they strike out?"

"S-southeast —"

That was all Girt Sasabe wanted. His bronc was clouting dust like a twister when he settled in the saddle. Matheson was shouting something but Girt didn't slow to listen — time enough for that when he got back with the fellow's daughter. And he'd come back with her, by grab! Else he'd not come back at all.

It made him writhe to think of loveliness such as hers in the hands of a man like Benson. Cow thief, tin horn, killer — the name had not been coined too foul to apply to Benson. Master schemer, brash with effrontery, he was overlord of all the rustlers. Every owlhooter in the Territory paid allegiance to the man; not one but split his swag with Benson or paid with his life for the oversight. And the worst of it was, Girt thought vindictively, not one lawman could get the goods on him.

"But things'll be different now," he promised. "He's gone too far this time. Snatchin' that girl will trip him!"

At the edge of town he cut for sign — found it. There were three of them. Benson, the girl and — "Yes," Girt nodded. "The third one will be Valmora."

Girt was new in this country, but the direction shoved by the fugitives could lead to but one conclusion — Lincoln. They were striking for the border, for the safety of Lincoln County. And it *would* be safe; none knew this better than Sasabe, who had come from there but a month ago. In the midst of a bloody range war, Lincoln had too many ills of its own to

17

worry over one trifling thing like a kidnaping at Broken Stirrup.

Girt recalled the whirl of events that had placed him in this saddle. Arrival in Broken Stirrup had been heralded by gunsmoke. Fresh out of the powder fumes of the Murphy-Chisum feud, Girt had drifted north in a search for quiet employment — a chance to live his life as others did without resort to Colt-butt. But that, it looked like, had been asking too much. Trouble had jumped right at him in the shape of "Anvil" Crispin, a rough, knife-packing Texican who'd had the whole town buffaloed. This Crispin it was who had killed their sheriff; but his toughness was not of a caliber to turn the load from Sasabe's Greener. "Get off that bronc!" yelled Crispin; and Girt had given him both barrels.

"Justifiable homicide," had been the coroner's opinion; and then Clay Matheson, who ran most things in the county, had gotten him appointed sheriff. Three days back that had been, though it seemed a good while longer. While they'd been pinning the star on his vest, Matheson had explained to Girt how rough it was for cow raisers to have a rustler like Cash Benson practicing his trade in the county. "Run him out or rub him out, an' they'll write you up in the histories!"

Girt didn't know about that, but he sure would like to oblige Clay.

He'd been three days at it now and was discovering that this Benson was no kind of a jasper to stamp your boot and yell "Boo!" at. He was a real double-acting engine and every crook in eighty miles addressed the man as "Boss."

Well, Benson was headed for Lincoln — no mistake about that part. Thought of the place brought up in Girt's mind the part he had played in its range war. On the Murphy-Dolan side he'd been till the Kid swapped over to Chisum. Not liking the cattle king's politics nor the way his tough bucks handled nesters, Girt's allegiance got a little mite tangled. According to *his* lights, Murphy and Dolan had the right of things; but his admiration for the Kid — for young Bill Bonney — made thought of fighting against him almost a sacrilege. Seemed like the fair and the square of the matter had been to cut his stick and drift.

And that was exactly what he had done. He'd left Lincoln County to stew in its juice and gone perambulating north into Torrance. That had been all right. But here he was heading back again, lured on by a kidnaped girl!

What would young Bill Bonney say? Indeed, what would Murphy-Dolan? He guessed both sides would gun for him. The moon had a bloody nose tonight — there was apt to be thunder and lightning.

3

Midafternoon of the third day saw Girt pulling into Lincoln. He was by no means sure he was still on the trail, for sign had petered out yesterday. He was green at this business, but he had a capacity for learning that in the end might well make up for it. He could read a sign when there was any to be read; but for the last six hours there hadn't been any and he was reluctantly forced to the conclusion that this was not going to be any short chase. It was going to be a long one fraught with unpleasantness, hardships, danger; and it made him boil to think of Merrilyn Matheson being compelled to travel with men like Valmora and Benson. He dared not ponder her fate should he fail to overtake them. He muttered doggedly: "They've got to be here — *got* to!"

He entered Lincoln leisurely, warily, eyes skinned and taut nerves singing. This was the Lincoln feud's stamping ground and woe to the man who got careless! Woe to himself, Girt thought, if certain tough Lincolnites spied him; for there were no olive branches being passed around. Hot lead was the only thing free.

And there'd be plenty of them willing to give him that — Bob Ollinger, for one; and maybe even Bill Bonney. Leaving Lincoln like he had, both sides might be hunting his scalp!

He rode in from the north — though not by the trail, and approaching Murphy's Big Store saw something that slimmed his eyes down — saw it yonder in front of McSween's. A double column of blue-coated, black-faced cavalry all drawn up in a line and with a gatling's black snout pointed square at the lawyer's door. And yes! By grab, there was old Nanny-Goat Dudley himself! Brass-collar dog of the military!

Something was up and no mistake, and Girt urged his bronc forward curiously just as a cheering bunch of gun-toters came piling out of Murphy's. Out of the store they came; through its doors and some even vaulting from its windows. And they came spilling from the hotel, also; every jack grinning.

They sure were tickled about something. Flick Farsom saw him and yelled: "Hi,

Girt! Come back to see the pay-off?" And Old Man Pierce dragged him off his horse and Andy Boyle like to knocked his teeth out clouting him on the back; and then Girt saw a face that wasn't grinning back at him — Bob Ollinger's.

The deputy marshal by his breath was liquored up more than usual and the glint in his eye spelled trouble. Girt's hackles rose as he watched the long-haired gun fighter advance; they had never cottoned to each other much and Ollinger, just before Girt had left this country, had allowed he would hang Girt's hide on the fence.

Girt thought about that now. "You comin' for that hide?" he asked; and invective poured from the marshal.

The men around Girt backed away. But Girt didn't back. He stood in his tracks with a cold tight grin. Bob Ollinger eyed him darkly.

"What you doin' back here? Didn't I warn you out?"

"Did you?" Girt said politely.

"More of your lip, eh?" Ollinger glared. "Git away from that horse! I bin needin' a new example!"

"Oh, come off it, Bob," Flick Farsom said. "He's just a kid. He ain't hurtin' no one —"

"He's a friend of that horse-stealin' Bonney brat an' by Gawd I owe him somethin' —"

"Sure," Girt said. "I remember, Ollinger. About ten dollars, ain't it?" And he grinned right into those flaming black eyes and laughed the way the Kid would. "But that's all right," he said airily. "You can keep it if you're broke —"

"Broke!" gritted Ollinger hoarsely. "By Gawd, boy, I'll break *you!*" he snarled, and started for Girt like he meant it.

But Girt, aping Bonney again, just stood there and grinned at him boldly. "Speakin' of breaks," he said, "you sure hit lucky I had to leave town in a hurry. I hear you been throwin' your jaw around that you run me out of the country. Cry-*minie!* Was you fishin' for some kind of a belly-laugh?"

Old Man Pierce ducked back of the horse trough and from the corner of his eye Girt saw Andy Boyle trying to flatten himself back of a young cottonwood.

They had reason.

Ollinger had lashed himself into a fury. His right hand clawed for the gun on his hip.

Girt Sasabe moved like lightning. Took a long step forward and drove a left hook that rattled Bob Ollinger's teeth. The marshal, spitting blood and oaths, got his gun — got it out and clear of leather. But before he could trigger, Girt hit him again and he sat down hard in the dust.

"What you waitin' on?" Girt taunted.

Eyes blazing, the marshal surged to his feet, but again Girt proved himself faster. Ollinger, crouched for a spring, found himself staring down Girt's sawed-off Greener.

"You was sayin' —" Girt drawled with all of the Kid's brash insolence.

"Sayin' he's got enough, I guess!" Flick Farsom said with a chuckle. Old Man Pierce loosed a snicker then and the whole crowd burst out laughing. With cheeks beet-red, the marshal snatched up his gun and went slinking off down a side alley.

Andy Boyle slapped Girt on the back. "That was tellin' him! He sure understands *that* language!"

Girt shoved the shotgun back in its boot. He was glad Ollinger had quit when he had; glad he'd taken his star off too, because Dolan's crowd mightn't 've liked it. And one thing was sure: he had enough on his hands chasing Benson, without engaging in private gun battles. "What's goin' on here, anyhow? Somebody gettin' married?"

"Naw." George Davis explained: "Ol' Dudley's goin' to read the riot act. Better trot along over an' hear it."

"Sure thing, boy. Judgment Day is here," Boyle boomed; so Girt went along to see.

These, Girt knew, eyeing the black horsebackers, were the buffalo troops from Fort Stanton, the garrison maintained in this out-of-the-way corner of the Territory to keep the Mescaleros mindful of the Golden Rule and the gifts of the Great White Father. But the presence of Dudley himself put an odd complexion on the business, for the colonel was brass-collar dog of the military and none but the most important of occasions could persuade him outside the fort's walls.

"What's up?" Girt called at Dad Peppin, the sheriff Governor Axtell had appointed for Lincoln after tying a can to old Copeland, the man McSween had shoved in at gun point. "What are all them horse soldiers here for?"

"Because I sent for 'em — that's what!" Peppin growled testily. "The owlhooters have plumb took this town over — for the last three days they've had us caged up like goldbirds, a-mockin' constituted law an' order an' braggin' they'll fill Boot Hill with our corpses. Had us outnumbered four to one; but you'll hear 'em sing diff'rent now!"

"Where's all the Murphy crowd?" Girt asked, squinting round.

"Dead! — leastways the most of 'em is. Them as ain't skun out! Murphy-Dolan's gone busted an' — *shh!*"

Girt, following the Lincoln sheriff's stare, saw Alex McSween stepping into his dooryard. The old rogue hadn't changed a heap, Girt thought. Little more gaunted up, perhaps, from the weeks he'd been in hiding; but otherwise much the same Mac he remembered. His Chinaman's mustache still hung straggly as ever and the martyr look was being paraded more than ever. And that flopsy, dog-eared Bible was still tucked under his arm.

McSween's men came out after him; fanned out in a loose half circle. They were grinning wide as Murphy's men, and, "Think Dudley's troopers have come to help *them*," Dad Peppin remarked to Girt dryly.

Each of McSween's crew packed a rifle. A tough and ornery looking bunch Girt thought them — except for the Kid; and even *he* showed less than his usual spruceness. He caught Girt's eye, chucked a grin and a wink and swaggered over to stand by tall Alex.

A brash, gay lad, Girt thought — the kind to charge hell with a bucket. He had known Bonney well in the old days; Evans, the Kid and himself and Flick Farsom had all chased cows' tails for John Chisum for forty per month and sour beans.

Girt wondered how the Kid could stand for McSween's high-handed arrogance, his schemes and pettifogging ways. Why, everybody knew Alex for a crook! But, like Benson, he was hard to get the goods on; and Girt guessed Bonney wasn't too particular. He knew for a fact the Kid regarded cow-thieving as something of a lark.

Then Girt's eyes were drawn to Dudley.

Shoving his chest out like a pigeon, the colonel said from the saddle: "Mister McSween, I'd like to know the meaning of this demonstration!" He said it like it was Lincoln practicing the Gettysburg Address.

Alex waved his Bible and glared at the colonel indignantly.

" 'Demonstration' is an apt description!" he growled bitterly. "Demonstration by a crew of lawless blackguards masking their connivings and persecution of a defenseless law-abiding citizen behind the tarnished shine of a sheriff's star!" And the look he shot at Peppin would have split a white oak post.

The colonel goggled. "Defenseless citizen? Law-abiding —"

"I'm talking," McSween declared, "about myself! You know very well I've not done anything to hang my head about. My only crime — if you can call it that —"

"Is stealin' the Fritz insurance money!" Andy Boyle piped up.

Dudley ignored him. So did McSween; though he could not very well have missed the boos and horse laughs that went up. But the colonel's scowl quickly quieted these. Leaning forward he said sternly: "Mister McSween, this fighting must cease at once!"

"I approve that sentiment heartily, sir," declared Alex, meek as Moses. "If you're referring to this unprincipled feud Major Murphy has dragged me into —"

"I am referring to this rioting and violence!" Dudley snapped. "It is an outrage, sir! I want it stopped at once!"

McSween bowed. "Unhappily," he pointed out, "I have no say in the matter —"

"You can turn those outlaws out of your house!" shouted Dudley apoplectically.

"What! — and leave myself at the mercy of James Dolan and his scalp-hunting understrappers? No indeed, sir," McSween shook his head with vigor. "Not on Wednesdays, Colonel! The Lord only knows how glad I'd be to see an end to this gunplay; but those Murphy ruffians won't let me — they'll never quit till we're all in our graves. If you want to stop this, talk to them! *Those* are the men responsible — Dolan and that star-packing Peppin!"

He might have said more but for the catcalls and hisses of the Store crowd. Dudley drew himself up stiffly. "I'm afraid that's hardly a disinterested opinion." He said then like Nero calling the tune for Rome: "You've my orders, Mister McSween — defy them at your peril."

Girt abruptly lost interest in the wrangle as, glance roving, his eyes took in a business that grabbed for his full attention. Flick Farsom was shoving out of the crowd and Old Man Pierce was following him. And farther over, sauntering blithely in the same direction, was the loud-mouthed gun fighter, Boyle. Girt knew them all; knew they were heading for Murphy's hotel. They were the toughest of Murphy's hombres; and on the steps of the old hotel stood Murphy's partner, Dolan — boss of the Murphy fighters. His mouth held a nasty smile.

Be uncommon odd, Girt thought, if

there were nothing in the wind.

He made up his mind in a hurry. This was not, strictly speaking, his business; but it strained his curiosity mightily and he urged himself on with the thought that these fellows might have knowledge of Benson — perhaps of the rustler boss's whereabouts. And any straw, however slim, must be seized if he were to save Clay Matheson's daughter; there was no getting around *that* part!

Soon as they went inside the hotel, he took a roundabout way past the soldiers and sauntered up to the hotel himself. He heard no sound, neither voice nor movement; heart thumping, he stepped inside.

He heard the mutter of voices now, all right; Farsom's protesting, and Dolan's, suavely arguing. Heard Dolan say: "You leave me be the judge of that," and then the scuff of diminishing boot sound.

They were out back someplace, Girt thought; and eased across to an open window.

Yes. There they were, over by the chopping block. Dolan was giving orders and the others, each with a basket, were scooping up chips and sawdust. But it was what Jim Dolan was holding that turned Girt's eyes darkly narrow. A tin cup was in

31

his left hand and his right held a coal-oil bucket!

So *this* was what they were up to while Dudley's hot air claimed the attention of McSween and his partisans. It made Girt's hackles rise, the thought of what this sight portended. They were fixing to start a fire and he didn't need to ask whereabouts, by grab! They sure weren't aiming to burn down Murphy's hotel!

Girt whirled at a slight sound back of him, the hair on his neck climbing higher. Jack Long, teeth bared, stood behind him; and the look of those teeth wasn't pleasant. Nor did it ease the cramp of Girt's muscles, the way Long's hand was splayed by his gun butt. "Oh-oh!" Long breathed very softly. "A spy, eh? Caught in the act!"

The roof of Girt's mouth was too dry for words. Long had him, and dead to rights. The gun on Girt's hip might as well have been a pea-shooter; he packed it for show more than anything, and did not try to kid himself he could stack against this kind of hombre.

"Don't let me interrupt you," Long said nastily. "Go right on with it — turn around like you was, you scissor-bill —"

"Turn around yourself!" said a new voice, purring; and Girt nearly fell through the floor. For he'd know that voice in ten thousand! — the scathing scorn of Darinthy-May Tolliver!

Questions clawed at his mind like a bobcat in a hound pack. But he had no time to find answers. "Get his gun, Girt," the Honky-Donk's proprietress bade coldly. "Fine! Now take them piggin strings off his belt an' tie him in a tangle. . . . Good. Shove your bandanna in his mouth an' let's git out of here."

Girt lost no time in following that last suggestion; this was no place to be found were Dolan to come inside again — nor would he care to be found any other place by a Dolan man once this guy got his tale told. So far as relations with the Store crowd were concerned, the sooner he got out of Lincoln the longer his health would last.

"I did give you credit for a *little* sense," Darinthy-May told him hotly just as quick as they got outside. "You make me tired, Girt Sasabe! Chasin' 'way over here after that fool girl! You ought to be —"

"Well," Girt muttered, cheeks burning, "what did *you* chase over here for?"

She gave him one blasting look, swung around and went off like a pot-leg, looking mad enough to smack the devil with his horns on.

"Cry-*minie!*" Girt growled, staring after her. "Now what's got into *her* craw?"

But the stress of more urgent matters soon turned his thoughts away from her. Dolan was going to set McSween's house afire in an effort to dislodge the gun fighters sheltering behind those thick mud walls. Girt couldn't rightly blame him, knowing something of the story back of this feud. McSween and Chisum, greedy for power and its by-products, had tried by every means at their command to force the Store Company out of business, to ruin Murphy and Dolan and run them out of the country. That the scheme had misfired and put themselves in a hole was damned well good enough for them, he thought. They had stopped at nothing — not even murder; and now the law had caught up with them and they deserved everything they got for it. But the devil of it was Bonney'd get it, too — and Billy the Kid was different!

He wasn't like Bowdre, and French and Middleton, Wayte and all those others who were working their triggers for pay and took their loot where they could get it. He was entitled to more consideration if only for his bravery which, in a land where courage was taken for granted, was everyplace a byword. Besides, he wasn't really an outlaw; leastways, not an outlaw at heart. The price they'd put on his scalp had come by way of defending his principles. He'd been a staunch friend of British John Tunstall's — Tunstall, the San Felice rancher who'd gone into pardners with McSween and, because of his misguided allegiance, had been gunned to his death by a posse.

No, the Kid was different — didn't Girt *know* it? He'd not eat and slept with the Kid that year they'd punched cows for John Chisum without discovering something of the Kid's character. A fine fellow and a saddlemate who'd give the shirt off his back for a friend. And a pal was a pal no matter which side of the face he happened to be riding on now! The blame for Billy's outlawry lay squarely with Brady's posse who had downed John Tunstall like he was a rattler! *That* was what had planked Bill Bonney's boots in this bloody trail he followed — that oath he'd sworn to "get every man" responsible for the death of his English friend.

Of course, this wasn't finding Merrilyn Matheson; but a friend had some rights to consideration, too; and Bonney needed warning badly or he'd be trapped at

McSween's like those others.

There wasn't any way around it; he would have to warn Bonney — and quick!

Standing by the tie-rack Girt, salving his official conscience with the thought Bonney might know of Benson's whereabouts — or at least one of his hideouts to which the girl might have been taken — racked his brains for some way of getting in touch with him without the thing being too public; because after all he was a lawman now and had no business gabbing with outlaws.

But think as he would and did Girt could find no way but the obvious. Dudley's troopers with their nickering, stamping horses held the roadway. Murphy-Dolan men fringed that blue-clad column like the feathers in a tall buck's hair; and over across, trampling down the reds and yellows of Mrs. Alex's flowers, McSween's tough crew stood lounging on their rifles. They had grinned first off; but now the grins were gone, their faces warped to black scowls by the tone of Dudley's sermon. Darker and bleaker grew the look of Bonney's stare; and Girt knew that if he were to warn the Kid he had better be about it.

McSween and circumstance, and

McSween's hard-riding owlhooters, had dealt the Store Company its death-blow. The firm was smashed — was bankrupt, and Murphy, head of the combine, was in a Santa Fe bed from which he was destined never to rise. The company's backers were scattered, many of them going into hiding lest they fall prey to the Kid's fast-shooting rifle. Tunstall was dead and buried and John Chisum was still behind bars in the old Las Vegas lock-up. *This was pay-off;* final curtain to the range war — and already the cards were dealt. McSween and Chisum had won; but they must pay the price, and unless Girt warned him swiftly, the Kid must pay it with them.

For fifteen months the Kid had been Girt Sasabe's ideal; his pattern of what a man should be, of how a man should conduct himself. Every act of the Kid's was seen by Girt through a mist of heroic glory. He knew what the Kid would have done in his place; so clenching his jaws he did it — started hotfoot for McSween's.

4

He felt the stares of John Kinney and two-three others of the Murphy men fall upon him with a brittle impact as he started across the street. He felt the gooseflesh crawling on his neck but he'd made his mind up now; he was going to warn Bill Bonney and he held steadily to his course. An edge of his glance, held straight ahead, saw Peppin wheel, throw a look of speculation at him; but the Lincoln sheriff did not speak.

Someone else did though — Jesse Evans, the biggest Dolan straw boss. He stepped from the crowd into Sasabe's path and planted himself there solidly. And the grin he showed Girt wasn't fooling anyone. "Where away?" he asked. "Not leavin', sonny?"

The goosebumps grew on Sasabe's neck though his cheeks flushed at the appellative. He was forced to pull up, for the other wouldn't budge; and his eyes were bright with warning. Had it been someone else, Girt would have clouted him down — but a man didn't clout Jesse Evans. Not if he was in his right mind he didn't. Evans was held the most dangerous man on Dolan's payroll. Girt knew him well as he knew Bill Bonney, for they'd all punched cows for Chisum in the old days and had been considered friends. But if there was friendship in Evans now, his look held nothing to show it.

"What's the matter, son? Cat got your tongue?" Evans' drawl was mocking. "Just where was you fixin' to go, boy?"

"I — well, I —" Girt hesitated. Seemed like a lump had got jammed in his throat. Tiny flecks of flame were coalescing in Evans' stare. He had his hands in his pockets; but Girt remembered having seen them there before and a man falling dead split seconds later. Every curve of the gun fighter's frame growled menace.

Girt's roving glance picked up Flick Farsom and Andy Boyle sifting into the crowd to the left of him and knowledge of what their return portended made him desperate. "What the hell is it to you?" he grunted, and was surprised at the huskiness of it. He could feel men's glances boring into him and the sudden quiet spreading ripple-like through the gathered watchers.

But Evans smiled, a thin, tight-lipped little smile that chased a chill up Girt's spinal column. He tried to think what the Kid would have done; and abruptly inspiration came to him.

But too late!

Like it was a signal, a trooper cut loose with his bugle. Came a rattle of arms and a stamping of horses as the blue column straightened its line. A command rang out and the soldiers jabbed up their broncos. The bugle blared again and the long double line started moving like a sluggish snake uncoiling.

"Looks like the show is over, boy. Come along an' I'll buy you a drink," Evans said, and tucked his hand inside Girt's arm.

Girt hung back, a chaos of indecision riding him. A look across Evans' shoulder disclosed the McSween adherents filing back inside their barricades — showed the Kid going into McSween's. Evans' smile showed grimly knowing at the look on Girt's young cheeks.

"Just as well, boy," he drawled softly. "I sabe how you feel about Bonney — felt that way myself once. But it's no good; he's a bad 'un. And won't never get no better."

Girt pulled loose with a scowl. "He's a damn swell guy!" he cried hotly. "A heap too good for what they've got planned to happen to him — don't parade any lies for me! Just because he's working his guns for McSween, you've all got a mad on him — you want to kill him like a wolf!"

"That's right," Evans answered grimly. "Like a wolf — which is what he is. A sneakin' coyote wolf."

Before Girt thought — so swift, so instinctive was his loyalty — his fist lashed out and crashed against Evans' jaw. The force of the blow staggered Evans, rocked him back on his heels, white-cheeked. But he kept his feet. He stumbled back a step and stood there thoughtfully rubbing his jaw.

Girt could see the effort the man put forth to keep his hand clear of his gun butt.

He said: "I — I —"

Abruptly Evans turned on his heel, strode away with his head held stiffly. And none of the crowd who had seen what had happened dared look till after he passed them.

It made Girt feel pretty cheap some way. And he didn't feel no better about it as one by one the others turned around and went tramping off after the gunfighter. He knew Evans could have killed him; could have had a gun smoking before his own draw even started. He halfway wished Evans had. Almost anything, Girt felt, would have been easier to bear than the contemptuous way the Dolan straw boss had left him. Like he was a kid caught stealing candy.

Then let them think what they liked, he thought; damn them! But the defiant look he stabbed round was wasted. No one had hung round to see it.

He felt more ornery than ever staring at nothing but departing backs. "Hell with 'em!" he snarled in a passion. "The Kid's all right — he's a first-rate fellow — the only square-shooter around! An' by grab I'll love to prove it!"

Then he remembered the trap they'd got rigged for Bill Bonney and the thought of it near made him sick. They didn't want to know what a fine fellow Bill was — all they wanted was to see him dead so they could split up the reward money.

A bunch of buzzards. A bunch of stinking scavenger buzzards — that's what they were; the whole darn lot of them! But it ought to be Dudley could stop them. By grab, he'd put it up to the colonel!

Girt found Colonel Dudley gone into camp across from the church with his guns trained on the houses of Montana and Patron. The McSween men — mostly Mexicans — in those places were under the command of Martin Chavez, and Chavez was talking with Dudley when Girt came up. Or, to be more exact, the colonel was talking to Chavez.

"You see these guns?" Dudley barked at the Mexican.

"*Si*," Chavez nodded. "You 'ave come to protec' the town, no?"

"Should these guns go off," the colonel said, "they'd blow down those 'dobes and kill every man you've got in them."

Chavez smiled. "The *señor* makes the joke." He chuckled with Latin leisure. "Everyone knows you 'ave bring your soldiers for protec' the life an' property —"

"Exactly! And if those hombres of yours fire another shot I'm going to blast those houses into dust piles!" Dudley eyed the Mexican grimly. "I suggest you order your pelados to throw down their guns. And when they've done that, my further suggestion is that the whole works get themselves into their saddles and start looking for greener pastures. If that's not plain —"

Martin Chavez gaped. He stared at the colonel goggle-eyed. "You — you are commanding us to — to leave Lincoln?"

"I certainly am. And if you value your health you'll lose no time getting started."

Girt, shoving forward, caught the colonel by the arm. "Say — listen!" he exclaimed. "If you send these fellows away, that'll leave McSween and his friends —"

Girt's words fizzled out under Dudley's cold stare. "That is precisely my intention," the colonel said stiffly. "For Chavez's Mexicans to leave McSween and his outlaws plumb alone. If they leave at once I shall undertake to see that they're not fired on. Otherwise," he added sternly, looking Chavez menacingly in the eye, "I shall send a troop of cavalry to round up any that escape my bombardment and have them taken to the fort to await trial."

"Trial?" Girt found his voice. "Trial for *what?*"

"For aiding and abetting outlaws. For resisting duly authorized officers in pursuance of their duty. Come, come!" Dudley said impatiently. "Don't you realize Sheriff Peppin holds United States warrants for most of the men who are hiding in McSween's house?"

"But look," Girt cried. "The Kid —"

"Ah! That young rascal, sir, is the worst of the entire lot. Hanging's too good for him — he's a killer — a public menace. A mad dog; exactly what Brady called him. He ought to be boiled in lard!"

Girt went back a step beneath the colonel's glare. The vindictiveness of the irate officer's tone completely silenced him for the moment. That anyone could feel so strongly against young Bonney — a youth but barely turned nineteen — was amazing; amazing and alarming too, for it showed as plain as anything how public opinion had veered. When Girt had pulled out of the county, the Kid had been pretty much a favorite; even the Murphy men, who had every reason to hate and despise him for a bunch-quitter, had at that time accorded him a certain measure of tolerance. Now that tolerance was gone. Everywhere Girt Sasabe turned he found nothing but bitterest hatred. A single white-hot desire seemed to have warped men from their reason; a fierce and malignant craving to see Bill Bonney planted.

The colonel's voice finally pulled him from his thoughts. "You clearing out," he asked Chavez, "or have I got to smoke you out, sir?"

The Mexican shrugged with a Latin eloquence. He bowed. "We will leave, Excellency. Since it is your wish, we will leave at once — *muy pronto*. And your consideration," he said in Spanish, "will be like a bright light in our remembrance of this dark hour."

He bowed again with a Latin flourish and abruptly strode away.

The colonel with a grimace wheeled his bulk to stare at Girt. "As for you, young fellow, let me give you a piece of advice. I don't know who you are, nor do I give a tinker's dam; but if you want to get along in this country, sir, you'll do well to keep clear of Bonney —"

"But what's he done?" Girt cried. "Why has everyone turned against him?"

"Done!" Dudley stared like he thought Girt was loco. "Did you say *done,* boy? Why, Goddlemighty! if there's any crime he hasn't done I'd like to know about it!"

"You talk a heap like Dolan, mister," Girt began to say hotly; then he recollected who this Dudley was — the high mucky-muck of the military, the brass-collar dog of Fort Stanton. As he checked the rush of his words, the colonel's face went livid and he pulled him six inches straighter and he spluttered through his mustache: "Orderly! Orderly, place this fellow under arrest! *This instant!*"

Girt saw that he had gone too far and tried to smooth it over. "I'm afraid I spoke a bit hasty, sir. I apologize — now wait a second," he cried as the orderly grabbed for his arm: "I said I'm sorry an' —"

"You'll be sorrier," snapped the colonel bleakly, "before you're loose again. Orderly, put this man —"

"Hold on!" Girt muttered, staring. The McSween men under Chavez had filed out of Patron's place and Montana's; had heaped their weapons in a pile and now were getting aboard their horses, which a wrangler had brought up from behind Juan Patron's store. The men, if not all Mexicans, at least were dressed as such; vaquero-garbed with tight-fitting jackets, shotgun pants and tall, cone-shaped sombreros. Dusk was settling rapidly, yet even so, through the gathered shadows something had caught at Girt's attention, sharpening his eyesight. A face it was, a dark and hawklike face seen but for a fraction as the man swung into leather. But a face he knew — one he had good cause to remember. And those chaps with their studdings of turquoise and silver!

Yorba Joe Valmora! Girt would have taken his oath on it any place.

"Hold on —" he muttered, shoving forward. But the orderly grabbed at him roughly and with a swift move pinioned his arms. Struggling, Girt growled furiously: "I ain't tryin' to cut my stick! By grab, sir," he cried at the colonel, "there's a fellow over there I'm wantin'!"

"Oh, is there now?" Dudley's suave tones were sardonic. "I'm quite aware you're not cutting your stick. As for your wantings, my buck, I expect there's a number of things you'll be wanting ere long; and your freedom is like to be one of them. Orderly" — the colonel's voice took on a crispness not to be grinned at — "disarm this fellow and see that he's put in irons —"

"But hell's fire — look!" Girt gritted desperately. "You're talkin' at a lawman, colonel! I'm the sheriff of Torrance County! In that crowd over yonder that's fixin' to ride is a jasper I been hunting — Yorba Joe Valmora! He helped Cash Benson —"

"So you're hunting somebody now, eh?" Dudley looked Girt up and down like a bronc fetched out for a horse trade; and laughed. Dry as sandpaper scraped on tin he said: "A pity you didn't think of it sooner! As for that other lie — it happens I've some friends in Torrance County and I don't consider them brainless enough to go electing any beardless boy to the

48

shrievalty." His scathing glance rubbed across Girt's vest. "Where's your star — or are you travelin' incognito like those English dukes that come over here flaunting their airs in our faces? Never mind!" he growled, holding up a hand. "You can tell me all about it after I've settled this crazy feuding. Orderly —"

But Girt had got enough of it. A quick tug broke him loose. An outlashing fist left the orderly jackknifed and gasping. For he was surer than ever now it had been Valmora he had seen; and while the colonel had been exercising his talking talents, someone among those mounting Mexicans had struck a match to fire his cornhusk cigarro and its light had shown a turning head whose face had been etched in young Girt's mind from the moment he first saw it. Though a steeple hat hid away her curls and her curves were lost in the rags of a wood peddler's clothing, her features, stained as they were and twisted with fright, could not be altered; and the vaquero's match limned them sharp and clear — the face of Merrilyn Matheson!

Already the mounted Mexicans were getting under way; and with a muttered oath Girt took out after them. The colonel's shout rode high and clear; calling for a sergeant, blast him! Girt sprinted harder. But as though the colonel's words were a spur, the horses of Chavez's men shook into a sudden gallop, clouting off into the deep-banked shadows. With a sobbing curse Girt ran like mad; and tripped on a root as a bugle blew. And before he could get up they were onto him.

5

It was one of the darkest moments of Girt's career when they hauled him up in front of the colonel. Trussed like a turkey bound for the baking, he was bleeding from a score of wounds, one sleeve of his shirt hung on by a thread and there was a nasty gash above his left eye where a trooper's clubbed carbine had struck him.

Dudley fixed him with a jaundiced stare. "Well, well!" he said through his nose. "That was quite a display you put on, Sheriff!"

Girt glared back at him sullenly. But he had learned one thing: When dealing with the boss of Fort Stanton, the less a man said the better.

The colonel turned away with a snort. "Put him in irons and remember this — if he gets loose again you'll regret it!"

As they were lugging him off Girt heard a commotion. Wrenching his neck in a backward look he saw that smoke was pouring from Alex McSween's and the colonel was doing a war dance. A wagon came rattling up behind a team of squealing buckskins. The brack-blocks snarled and the colonel bounced in. The trooper swung his whip with a long, savage grin and they were off like they were riding for Sheridan.

"Git on, you!" the sergeant snapped, and poked Girt's ribs with his rifle.

They took him to a little tent that had been thrown up back of Dudley's. They shoved him inside and the sergeant personally tied up the flaps. Girt heard them stamp off, but they left him a guard; he could see the fellow's shape. It was thrown against the tent wall by the fire from up the road.

Well, the Kid wouldn't be needing any warning from him now; he could see for himself what was coming. That was not much consolation for a man as young as Girt, though. He gritted his teeth and the nails of his clenched fists dug his palms as he reviled the colonel's ancestry. He gave up the pastime after a bit and tried a spell of wriggling to see if his bonds might give way. They didn't. Under the sergeant's watchful eye, the troopers had made an A-1 job of it. Sure looked like he was due to cool his heels a while. It might even, he thought darkly, be that Dudley would send him up to Siberia for life. Or some other place equally unpleasant.

His was not an enviable plight; and the divers and sundry sounds exploded through the night did little to make his position more bearable. After a while the sergeant came back with a cross-eyed little man who put some leg-irons on him; after that, all he had for company were his own glum fancies and the recurrent alarms that rent the night.

Along toward midnight — it may have been earlier — a rattle of shots broke out and jerked him upright like a touch of the sergeant's bayonet. The crash of firearms lasted intermittently for half an hour or so. Then things hunkered down a while and Girt could hear the wind plowing through the mesquite and greasewood, plucking gustily at his tent. And through each lull the crackling flames from over yonder where McSween's house burned brought to mind the roaring of the Pecos during spring flood.

Then, of a sudden, the gun blasts started up again and he guessed by the yelling and the shouting that McSween's trapped killers had at last been prodded into making a break for it.

It sure was hell, he thought imbitteredly, this being chained up like a dog. Both arms from elbow joints to fingertips had gone to sawing wood long since and now were numb as a gambler's heart and he was getting cramped all over. His gun was gone and they'd even taken his spurs, so it looked pretty much like he'd stay here.

But his mind kept churning, digging up and discarding divers plans to get him free. For Girt was young and hope was strong and his need to get loose was urgent. Every minute he was held cooped up saw Benson and Yorba Joe taking Merrilyn Matheson farther and farther away. They would dig deep into the wilds, he knew; into some hidden mountain pocket where one rifle could hold off an army.

It wasn't a jubilee prospect for a newly elected sheriff!

Abruptly he heard a scuffle of steps and the clump of boots stopped by his tent. A mutter of voices told of the newcomer in converse with the guard; and Girt in a sweat of impatience awaited the result of their parley.

It was but a matter of seconds in coming. A lantern flared up and somebody threw back the flaps of the tent. A man bent his shoulders and entered and when he looked up Girt saw by light from the lantern the guard had hung to the tentpole that though this fellow wore a dragoon's cap he was not dressed like a soldier. He might, Girt thought, be a scout of some kind; he was nobody Girt had seen before.

They studied each other in silence. Then the man's lips cracked a grin. "The Kid," he said, "got clean away — I figgered you might want to know."

Girt's heart gave a leap. "Got away? Say — that's swell!"

"Maybe so, — but you don't have to tell the General," the man said dryly. "Yep; he got plumb clear. But they got McSween and four-five others. The fight's all over — so's the war, I guess likely. McSween busted Murphy-Dolan; but now McSween's dead an' Tunstall's dead an' there's nobody left but Chisum an' Dolan an' neither one of 'em's much apt to keep this thing goin'. I guess Chisum's got what he wanted, even if he *is* still in jail. He won't be long, I'll bet that much — bet he'll have himself loose in a day or two."

Girt said: "Well, it's no skin off my nose. I got troubles of my own without sheddin' no tears for John Chisum. What's the lay, fellow? How come you to be bustin' in here?"

The man considered him with a long and reticent regard, the lantern light throwing dark shadows around his eye-sockets, bringing his hooked nose out like a vulture's beak. There was something smacking of vultures in the stoop of the jasper's shoulders too, Girt thought as he stared back sullenly. "I ain't on exhibition," he said grumblingly, "so if you've unloaded what you came for, suppose you hit the trail."

The man's thin lips showed a meager grin. "Gritty as fish eggs rolled in sand, eh? You showed some spunk, boy, talkin' up to the General that way. Got any notion what's goin' to happen to you?"

Girt glowered but kept his mouth shut.

"I don't mind tellin' you," the fellow said, "that you're in for a spot of trouble. Old Nanny-Goat Dudley ain't the man to take his dignity lightly. An' the way this feud turned out — his part in it, I mean — ain't goin' to make him feel no better. Special when report of it gets to Washington. He's goin' to start huntin' for a hound to kick —"

"If you ain't got nothing better to do," Girt grunted, "I have. Go roll your hoop an' clear out of here."

The man regarded him slanchways.

"Don't spit in the face of Providence, boy. You want to git out of this, don't you?"

Girt peered at him closer and something he read in the shine of the man's eyes checked the oath that had jumped to his lips. There was calculation in the man's rawboned cheeks; something sly and suggestive in his posture.

"You fixin' to get me out?"

"I could," the man said, "— for a price, boy."

"Then you're wastin' your time," Girt said gruffly. "I ain't got —"

"I'm not speakin' of money, boy." The man spread his hands and his grin showed the dull glow of teeth. He considered Girt while thoughtful-like he got out the makings and with an expert flick of the fingers rapidly twisted a cigarette. Leaning forward he put it in Girt's mouth and lit it with a match scratched on his thumbnail. Then he rolled himself a smoke; and after a couple puffs said: "There's things that's needin' doin', boy; an' come that you could do 'em. . . ." He paused, eyed Girt suggestively.

When Girt said nothing, the man remarked, "You told the General you was sheriff of Torrance County — that right?"

"That's what I told him."

"I mean" — the man's grin widened — "*are* you?"

"And if I am — ?"

"If you are, you're the lad I'm lookin' for." He put his left hand forward, turned it so the palm was up, and Girt's eyes narrowed abruptly. On the middle finger flashed a wide ring's mounting: a little flat slab of turquoise set in curiously twisted silver, native silver of Navajo working. Girt had only seen one ring like it; and his heart banged like a hammer. "Where'd you get that?" he cried softly.

"Ah!" the fellow grinned at him. "I see you know it. So let's get down to brass tacks. Our friend's kind of wishful of lyin' low for a spell till some of this feud stuff blows over — not that he's afraid, you understand, but 'cause he don't cotton to doing more killing than he has to. He figures if he gets out of the county for a spell, some of the animosity against him will ease off a little. Now here's the proposition." His voice took on a brisk note now and Girt glanced at him uneasily. "If you'll agree to hide him out for a spell, I'll undertake to get you loose of this." And he smiled at Girt like all he asked was the loan of a cigarette.

But Girt didn't do any smiling. His eyes

clouded over with worry and he wished he'd never seen this guy; or the ring on the fellow's third finger. He knew whose ring that was, all right; it belonged to young Bill Bonney!

He liked the Kid — he admired him a heap. But it seemed like this was asking a mighty big favor. After all, the Kid was an owlhooter with a big reward on his scalp. And Girt was sheriff — a *brand new* sheriff; and it wouldn't look good for him to be giving official shelter to an outlaw.

Bonney's messenger seemed to read his mind. "Why, hell!" he scoffed. "Who's goin' to know? You don't have to get out no *hand*bill! All our friend's askin's that you lay off his bunch —"

"His *bunch!*" exclaimed Girt, staring blankly. "Is he figurin' to —"

"Oh, just a few of the boys," the fellow said easily; "just three-four of his closest friends. Course, he *could* go to Fort Sumner — he could hide out up there. Was plannin' to, in fact, till he lamped you out in that crowd this evenin'. Then it come to him like a flash. You was his friend; mebbe *you'd* fix him up. He give me this ring an' told me to see if you'd do it."

"Well . . ." Girt hesitated, flushed and unhappy, torn between conflicting loyalty and admiration for the man he esteemed above all others and the cold obligations put upon him by his newly sworn oath. It was a sore dilemma for a man young as Girt to be faced with. No matter which he did — help Bonney or cling strictly to the letter of his oath — his position would be untenable — would saddle him with woe. No matter which he did, it seemed, he would never be able to look himself in the eye again.

"All you got to do," Bonney's messenger told him, "is to keep your lip tight-buttoned an' tend to your own business. Hell — is that such an awful lot for a guy to ask of a friend? Nobody's goin' to know he's hid out in your bailiwick — nobody that matters, anyway. Hell's bells!" he said impatiently, "what kind of feller are you? If you was in the Kid's fix now, he'd do as much for you an' think nothing of it. All you have got to do —"

"Well, listen —" Girt muttered, weakening. "If it gets out he's there an' my hand gets forced, I'll have to —"

"Sure! In that case you'll have to go after him. He's thought of that," the man said, smiling, "and told me to tell you he understands. In fact, he said if your hand gets forced, he'll pull out an' drop down to

Mesilla." The fellow's sharp eyes stabbed at Sasabe's face. "Then you'll do it?"

"Not so fast," Girt said. "I got to think this over." But he breathed more freely now, and though he still didn't cotton to such two-faced work, he knew in his heart he would do it. He scowled and glowered a spell, then finally said: "All right. Starting gettin' these dang things off'n me."

The man looked down at his leg irons and rasped a hand across his jowls. "Better leave them on a bit." He said dubiously: "I'll go have a talk with the colonel —"

"The deal's off, then," Girt said with an oath. "That fossil will see me in hell first!"

The man stood undecided and scowled. Then his eyes lit up and he clapped Girt's shoulder jovially. "Buck up!" he said. "I'll have you out of them quick as a cat laps whiskers," and before Girt could question him further, he ducked through the flap and was gone.

He was back inside three minutes and, stooping by Girt's hunkered form, he reached out and there was the scrape of steel on metal. The left iron fell off and then the right and Girt started up. But he dropped back quickly with a muttered curse. His legs were asleep from the knees on down and the man set to work on them roughly.

"Where'd you get the key?" Girt questioned.

"Now don't let that fret you," the fellow said shortly. "Be thankful I got it and shut up before somebody hears us." And he went on rubbing Girt's legs.

After a minute Girt shoved him aside and got up. His limbs were stiff and cramped and his wrists and feet felt like somebody was jabbing needles in them. "What about this rope?" he growled, in a hurry to be gone. "Ain't you got no knife?"

"Sure," the Kid's messenger said, and sliced the piggin strings off like butter. "Let's get out of this now before some fool falls over that sentry. Now don't," he added with a hand on Girt's arm, "act like you've got loose from a chain gang. Shove out your chest an' act like you're Dolan or someone."

Mention of Dolan sent a qualm through Girt, but he followed the man from the tent. The war was over; Dolan could look out for himself — he usually had, Girt remembered. Anyhow, what had Dolan done for him? It was help from the Kid that had freed him and it was up to him now to reciprocate.

62

"Where is he?" Girt asked as, arm in arm and wabbling like two convivial spirits lately crept from beneath some table, they swayed up the road toward Murphy's. "Is he waitin' for us someplace?"

"Not him!" the fellow answered. "He's a long ways gone from here, you bet you. But we'll find him. Keep your shirt on. You got a horse around here someplace?"

"Ought to have if someone ain't hooked him." Girt rasped his beard-stubbled jaw reflectively. "Let's see. Believe I left him 'longside the hotel there somewheres — yeah! that's him over yonder."

They steered a course toward an alley where a bronc's dark shape loomed vaguely. "You got good eyes," the fellow commented. "I hope you got as good a remembrance — Bonney'll sure go wild if you cross him!" And he stared at Girt kind of ominous.

Girt glared back with resentment. "What you take me for, anyhow? I give you my word, didn't I? If my word ain't —"

"Oh, sure — sure!" the fellow said hastily. "I was just twittin' you, sort of. But what I said about Bonney is gospel. Don't never cross him if —"

"Who's this talking of Bonney?" a sharp voice queried suspiciously; and a tall shape stepped swiftly in front of them.

Girt stared; stared again, looking closer — and shock choked the breath clean out of him. The light was poor, but there was enough of it still coming from the dying fire of McSween's gutted house for him to see a great deal more than he wanted to.

The man before them with pistol in hand was Dudley's sergeant — the fellow whose troopers had tied him!

6

There was just one thing to do; and while
Bonney's hawk-faced messenger stood stu-
pefied, Girt did it. His reaching left jumped
a clamp on the sergeant's gun hand. The
gun went off, its spray of flame just missing
Girt's crouched shoulder. Before the
cursing officer could trip the trigger again, a
jolting right packed up from Girt's bootstraps lifted the sergeant clean off his heels.
He went down and didn't get up again. Out
like a ton of brick!

Jaw slack, Girt's hawk-faced companion
goggled. Then he shook the cramp from
his body and tossed back his head in a
laugh. "Slick work!" he remarked with a
chuckle. "I was just goin' to bat him
myself."

"Yeah — I noticed that," Girt said,
scooping up the sergeant's gun; and something in his tone wiped the grin from the
other man's face. The fellow's hard eyes
raked Girt bright and narrow; but Girt was
peering off up the street, his glance stab-

bing through the shadows as though his only concern was for what that shot might bring after them. As though that thought were in his own mind, the hawk-faced fellow said gruffly: "Get your bronc an' we'll cut our stick. My nag's down at the corner; I'll wait there — make it snappy." And off he went, the night gloom swiftly swallowing him.

Girt's lips curled somewhat looking after him. Then he shook his head and, shoving into the alley, felt around for his horse and climbed up into the saddle. He'd never thought much of the Kid's confederates and this fellow appeared a good sample. A shifty, twisty sort of a man it would pay to keep your eyes on. It must gripe the Kid pretty bitter, he thought, having to put up with that breed of scorpion. But he guessed the Kid had to use who was handy, and it took hard men for his kind of game.

Bonney would be sacking his guns now that the war was over, though; would be sending these fellows packing. The Kid didn't like this man-killing stuff; it was only that he'd passed his oath to down John Tunstall's murderers. He'd just about done it too, Girt thought — except that he hadn't got Mathews.

66

A sorry business, blood-letting. Girt's heart went out to Bill Bonney. A quiet-mannered sensitive kind of jasper the Kid had been in the old days when they'd punched cows together for Chisum. A boy who'd like to watch the play of sun and shadows over the range; who could sit in his saddle and listen for hours to the swish of the wind in the chaparral. He was a man who liked a good story and oft told them himself round the night fires. And generous as the day was long — in fact, Girt thought, a kinder-hearted fellow you'd seldom ever find. As though the Kid were beside him now he could hear that gay, rollicking laughter that had so charmed him in the old days.

Poor Bill! Girt shook his head sadly. He guessed they'd drained all the laughter out of him. A man couldn't find much to laugh at, he guessed, with all those dead men on his backtrail.

The hawk-faced man was waiting at the corner. He said irritably: "I'd about decided you'd cut your stick without me. What the hell were you doin' — kissin' Peppin an' Dolan good-bye?"

"Sure," Girt agreed politely; and they rode out of town strictly silent. Girt was a little surprised at the direction the man

67

took; this way lay the Bonito's Double Crossing. It was the way he had come from Torrance. Capitan and Carrizozo; and beyond Ancho and Claunch to the north lay Broken Stirrup. He wondered if that were their destination and, if so, whereabouts they would pick up the Kid. But he wouldn't ask. This fellow had the manners of a fish vendor; and just to hear his nasal E-string voice rasped Girt's nerves like a file. There are some guys a fellow can't talk to, Girt mused; and this Mercury of Bonney's was one of them.

He supposed he'd ought to feel a little grateful toward the man for getting him free of Dudley's clutches; he even tried to off and on, but found it more than he could cut. He just plain didn't like the fellow; didn't like his grin or eyes, nor the way he had his hair cut. And, anyways, the man had only been following out the Kid's orders; if any gratefulness were due, it was due, not him, but Bill Bonney. And when you came right down to it, there wasn't any due because the Kid had made a deal out of it — a trade for mutual benefit.

But Girt didn't quite believe that, either. He guessed that was this fellow's idea. The Kid would have got him loose anyway.

Maybe, Girt thought, the Kid had struck

out for the hills someplace. Perhaps he planned to wait for them up in the Jicarillas or up around Jack's Peak.

But that idea got busted pronto when, without even so much as a grunt to warn him, Girt's guide swung his horse dead right. Down a shaley wash they angled, the horses sliding and slipping till they struck the dry creek bed.

"Where the heck we goin'?" Girt asked; and the man said, "Capitans," shortly, and returned to his morose silence.

Girt turned that over in his mind for a while and didn't at all like the looks of it. Why hang so close to Lincoln and yet bargain for a hideout in Torrance?

"Did the Kid get hurt makin' his getaway?"

"They didn't even scratch him."

There was something mighty odd here someplace — uncommon odd, Girt told himself. It didn't make sense that a man bad hunted as Bonney had been should want now that the war was over, to hole up so close to the victors. "It don't make sense at all!" he muttered.

By rights the Kid should be trying to get as far away as possible. Sheriff Peppin — if he hadn't already — would soon have posses out scouring the country for him. And Bonney must know this — so why risk hanging around?

"Say!" Girt exclaimed. "Is he stayin' to kill Billy Mathews?"

The man's head swung around and his quick stare was probing — Girt could see that even by moonlight. But all he finally answered was: "Not that I been told about."

And after that they rode faster.

Yet even so it was nearly dawn before they got to the rendezvous.

They angled up a final draw that quit in a rimmed box canyon; and Girt, peering round in the cold gray light, grumbled, "Guess we must of beat 'em — don't see 'em around here noplace."

The man said nothing but kept his horse moving at a steady walk that without any wasted time was taking him closer to the yonder overhang. Girt stared. There wasn't anything over there but a few gnarled juniper and a thicket of tangled mesquite that looked half starved by the rocky soil.

"But if that hombre," Girt muttered, "figures to do his restin' up alongside that rattlesnakes' haven, I reckon I can rest there too." And, still muttering over the tight-mouthed reticence of Bonney's messenger, he urged his horse in the fellow's wake; fishing out the makings as he did so.

The canyon was perhaps fifty yards across and about a quarter of a mile in length. The hawk-faced man was heading straight across it. And abruptly an owl's hoot made the uncanny stillness more oppressive. A second owl hoot answered it — or maybe it was an echo that straightened Girt so stiffly in the saddle.

His blue eyes slimmed to questing slits; for while he'd been fiddling with his cigarette the taciturn guide had vanished. Completely and most mysteriously. Girt's glance hadn't left the fellow's back for more than three-four moments. But he was gone, right enough.

Baffled and scowling, Girt was glowering round and reaching for his Greener when he heard the fellow's laugh. "C'mon," the fellow's voice said, "what you waitin' on?"

Girt's glance squeezed down slimmer and he lifted the Greener from its boot. "Straight ahead," came the mocking instructions from his unseen guide. "An' shake it up a little, will you?"

Resentful and exasperated, Girt urged his bronc as directed — reached the junipers and, even though he'd guessed by now the fellow must somehow be someplace beyond them, was astounded to see the horse sign tracking squarely into the mesquite. And then he saw another thing: all the thorns had been carefully whittled off the brush around the hoof sign.

To Girt that meant something. It argued that this rendezvous was no new hide-out but a cache entirely familiar to Bill Bonney's owlhoot riders. No wonder Peppin's posses had failed to round the Kid up! While the lawman spent fruitless weeks beating brush along the Pecos, all the time that sly young rascal must have been forted up here in the Capitans. Girt wondered as he shoved through the brush if McSween had been here too.

Coming out on the trees' far side, he saw the wearer of Bonney's ring lounging negligently in the saddle before a cave's dark opening. Tall it was, and narrow like the entrance to a mine tunnel; black as pitch and with a cold dank breath that turned his thoughts uneasy. Had all this talk of Bonney been some tricky blind? It was, Girt thought, a mighty fine place for a murder; and he watched the hawk-faced grinner with a new and risen vigilance.

But, as though cognizant of his thoughts, the man said, "Brush your hackles down, boy, I ain't fetched you here for buzzard bait. Got a match about you handy? We better get a wriggle on. The Kid ain't fond of waitin'."

Girt reached him a match with his right hand hugging the Greener's trigger. But the fellow only grinned wider and, taking a candle from his bedroll, cupped his two paws and lit it. He held it out to Girt. "Here you are, boy. Pack this light if you don't trust me, an' you can watch every move I make."

"Pack it yourself," Girt muttered; "I wasn't weaned day before yesterday. A fine target I'd make with a light in my hand — tote it yourself if you want it."

The hawk-faced fellow guffawed; took the light and started ahead. Girt followed watchfully, his hand still clamped to the Greener. He wasn't too good with a pistol — average quick, perhaps, but a long ways from being expert. But with his hand on his sawed-off shotgun he felt tough enough to match anyone. "It takes real guts to mock a shotgun," Jesse Evans had told him one time; and Girt had taken the hint.

He followed Hawkface through a perfect labyrinth of black and slime-hung passages. He'd just opened his mouth to question how much farther they must go, when a sound of voices reached him and a dim oblong of light loomed ahead.

The tunnel's damp floor angled up now a bit, then abruptly took a steep plunge downward. The light was growing stronger when Hawkface snuffed out his candle and reached forth a hand to stop him. The man's face darkened at the alacrity with which the muzzle of Girt's Greener swung to catch him in its focus. He snorted softly, then pursed his thin lips; and the owl's hoot that next moment filled the passage was so lifelike, Girt had to grab a fresh hold on himself not to stare round for it.

The voice-sound choked off on the instant. Seemed like there was no sound left in all this timbered rat's den. Then an answering call drifted up to them soft as the breath of a bat's still passing. Hawkface hooted twice more and with a grin swung out of his saddle. "Mighty particular the Kid is that we get these signals right. Better hoof it 'less you're cravin' a headache," he said, and without more words led his horse off down the pitch.

Girt swung down; started to put his shotgun up, then suddenly changed his mind. "Better to be sure than sorry," he muttered. "No tellin' who's here nor their politics." Greener in his right hand, then, and the bronc's reins in his left, he strode warily after his guide.

The light grew stronger still and the passage took an abrupt turn right and there, square ahead, was the tunnel's end, and sunlight so bright it was blinding.

A quaking feeling grabbed at the pit of Girt's stomach as with Hawkface he came from the tunnel into the glare of a tiny pocket gouged from the peaks — a clearing tight and brittle with the shapes of waiting men. A wolf pack was what they looked like, and wolfpack-like they watched him; each hard face as lacking of expression as the hacked inscrutability marking the stolid wooden features of the wares Mex doll vendors peddled.

And then a voice cried suddenly: "Danged ef it ain't the ol' son himself — hoss-thief hat an' everything! H'are you, Girt? How's sheriffin'? Dog but it's good to see you! Where the hell's your star at? Don't tell me you've throwed 'em over?"

Like the flight of fog under upsailing sun, Girt could feel the hostility melting; could see a slight relaxing of the taut-held wolfpack faces. "Whew!" he said with fervence, and: "You're sure holed up like a loafer, Bill!"

A couple of the owlhooters laughed.

"Shucks, I *got* to be!" Bonney chuckled. "Only way I keep alive these days — what with half the sons of this territory out for the hairs of my scalp. But step up an' meet the boys. Fellas, this here's young Girt Sasabe — as sassy a sheriff as ever packed tin; he's a friend an' a hombre bueno, so treat him right an' mind your manners." He stopped and grinned around at them; and then, to Girt: "I guess you know this vinegarroon?" and Charlie Bowdre, the man he jerked his thumb at, grinned at Girt with a wink. "Hell, yes!" Charlie said. "I guess we've sampled as much of Ike's coffin varnish as anyone —"

"An' this," Bonney plowed on, indicating a strapping big fellow with beefy face and two guns strapped to his middle, "is Dave — Dave Ruddabaugh; he can do cute things with a playin' card, Girt, so keep your eyes skinned sharp at him. That there's Jim French; I expect you've seen him around — used to shake a spry leg at the ladies. Yonder buck in that go-to-hell shirt's Hendry Brown — slick with a rope as he is with the iron an' a first-rate man to tie to. An' the dark-faced Texican hidin' behind that cholla is John Middleton — one of the boys whose map grins at you from half the posts in the county. John's a big dog in financial circles — got run out of Austin for bustin' a bank. An' this fella here that fetched you will most generally answer if you shout 'Doc!' loud enough — Doc Scurlock's his handle, though his pills is a little mite hard."

Doc Scurlock — Hawkface — guffawed and slapped Girt on the back. "Kid's a great joker, boy — shake your saddle blanket out 'fore you use it."

"What's new up to Lincoln, Girt?" asked Bonney, grinning.

Girt grinned a little too then, feeling a sight more comfortable now that the ice had been broken. "I didn't leave much after you did," he said; "I expect we both heard it the same. I'm sure much obliged to you, Bill, for —"

"Well, shucks," the Kid said airily, "I'd of done as much for any guy. You'd of done the same for me. Us old Chisum boys has sure got to stick together — eh, John?"

And Middleton loosed a great guffaw.

"We was just fixin' to eat," Brown said hospitably. "Haul up an' put on a nose-bag."

So Girt did; although with some qualms that he choked down along with his beans. The scalding hot java brought tears to his eyes, but he swilled it down manful-like; and after the boys got finished they fished out their makings and built monuments to

Durham; and Bonney dug a pipe from his chaps pocket and handed it to Girt. "Little present I been savin' you," he said; and Girt felt proud as Lucifer.

But after a while, when one by one the others had lolled off to pound their ears in the chaparral and he'd got the Kid more or less to himself, Girt told him guardedly:

"I expect I can make out to put you up in Torrance for a spell; but you can't have the run of the range, Bill. I got to think of my position an' that oath I took when they pinned the tin on my shirt."

"Sure," Bonney said, looking thoughtful. "A man's first regard has got to be for himself —"

"It ain't that," Girt said, flushing; "it ain't my hide that's botherin' me. But them folks up in Torrance County done made me sheriff 'cause they figgered I was a man to tie to. They look for me to make the country safe for their women-folks an' kids; an' some of 'em mightn't cotton to it much if it was to get around I was —"

"Sure," Bonney said again. "I reckon to understand that, boy, an' I sure won't cause you no trouble, come I can help it. Might be a heap better all around was I to take the boys up to Fort Sumner. Place is pretty nigh deserted now the military's left it an' —"

"Hell's fire!" Girt declared, rousing up. "What kind of a varmint would I be to let you take a chance like that?" He scowled at his boot tops fiercely. "We've eat together, worked together —"

But Bonney dragged him down. "True enough, friend Girt — true enough," he said; "but you ain't beholden for my safety. I can sure look out for myself in any man's country. I wouldn't want for you to go into this without you had both eyes open. I'm a marked man these days — I ain't Bill Bonney any more. I'm Billy the Kid — 'mad dog' of Lincoln County!"

A little bitter, those words of his, maybe; but only a young fellow like Girt, who remembered him as he used to be, could fail to note their swagger — their raised-voice braggadocio.

"Mad dog," repeated Bonney, rolling the taste of it over his tongue. "That's what Bill Brady called me, an' it's a name that's bound to stick. Mark my words, boy — I'll git no rest so long as they've shells an' shootin' irons. They've got me pegged out for a killer an' they won't never quit till they've downed me."

"They're a parcel of thick-headed fools, then!" said Girt, rousing up with an oath.

"But Chisum —"

"He's bad as the rest," declared Bonney. "Never put no trust in a cattle king; it's you an' me an' other guys like us that's made John Chisum what he is — that's built him up this empire. But d'ye think the dog is grateful? 'You fight for McSween an' me in this,' he told me, 'an' I'll guarantee you won't lose nothing by it. When the smoke clears off an' we've peace an' plenty along the Rio Pecos, Kid, come hunt me up an' I'll have land and a straw boss's job rigged up for every buck in your outfit.' Them's the very words he used, Girt, an' —"

"But, heck," Girt said in protest, "a man can't rightly say we've peace along the river yet —"

"Not ever will have," Bonney cried scowling, "so long's I'm loose an' they can find 'em a fool to hunt me! Don't you *see*? I know too much of what's back o' this — they can't have me left to go talkin'! What I know, if I told it, would send Honest John up for life."

"You mean —" Girt gasped.

"Never mind what I mean, boy; the Murphy crowd claims it was the Fritz insurance business started this; an' McSween an' Chisum's been doin' a lot of hollerin' about the way the Murphys downed Tunstall — but I know what I know, an' it's somethin' else again that got the cards stacked for this feud. An' you ain't seen the end of it an' never will till Chisum gets me planted away an' —"

"Hell!" Girt said. "You're all worked up, Bill; I 'low you're readin' 'er slanchways. I ain't takin' up for Chisum none, but I got to say you're paintin' 'er uncommon creepy. This'll blow over —"

"Don't never think it," the Kid snarled grimly. "Folks'll get up a lather over this for years! All it'll take to set 'em off is mention of one thing or another like Tunstall's killin' or that Blazer's Mill business or —"

"You sure got it on the brain," Girt told him; and stared at the Kid morosely. He was amazed and shocked to hear Bill Bonney take on so. "You lie low a spell," he said, "an' you'll find things lookin' a heap diff'rent. In five-six months all this hate'll cool off — why, hell! you'll prob'ly be a *hero*, Bill, with guys writin' songs about you —"

"A hero! Yeah — I'll look cute with wings on!" Bonney snorted. "You can have your harps an' haloes. I ain't going' to last much longer, I reckon — just ain't in the cards. Don't get the idee I'm complainin', but some smart buck'll slap a slug in my back or one of these pot-lickin' hounds mebbe" — his eyes slammed a look round the chaparral — "will stick a knife in my guts while I'm sleepin'. Nope — don't talk that stuff at me, son; money's a mighty temptin' thing. An' a price on your head is a power no man can reckon with. I'm goin' to have my fun while I can!"

"You mean —"

"Just that. Let the chips fall where they will!"

Girt said uneasily, "Thought you was wantin' to hide out a spell over in Torrance . . . ?"

"Sure. If it won't put you out too much, that's what I been figgerin' on doin'. But, first, there's a chore right here at Lincoln I got to get off my chest."

And Girt, seeing that pale blue flame of wickedness in Bonney's cold, lean stare, got a sudden hunch. "Cry-minie!" he said slow, kind of hoarselike. "You're stayin' to get Billy Mathews!"

7

Bonney stared, glance bright as a rapier; then suddenly he laughed.

"Mathews, eh? Well, no," he said; "I'd near forgot that pelican. Oh, I'll drop him if I can, all right, for his part in killin' John Tunstall. John was square as a die, Girt — the only fellow I could call my friend; an' they killed him like a rattlesnake because he had took up for me!" Then, his anger cooling a little, he said: "No, I wasn't thinkin' of Mathews; nor Peppin, either, blast him! I'm stickin' around to — but never you mind; you'll be hearin' quick enough when the time comes!" He looked up at Girt then; very cool and abrupt, his glance crack-thin. "What brought you back here, boy?"

Girt didn't much like the look of his eye; but like the Kid's dark hints about Chisum, he put it down to the state of Bill's nerves. Fishing out the carved-bowl pipe the Kid had given him, he fetched a light up from his boot sole. "Well, I'll tell you," he mumbled; "when I cut my stick I hadn't no thought of comin' back, but —"

"But when they made you sheriff at Broken Stirrup," said the Kid, wire-sharp and nasty, "an' pinned their tin to your shirt, you got all swelled up with big notions. You knew where you could lay hold of me an' the price they'd put on my pelt —"

"That's a ornery lie," yelled Girt, rocking up on his feet; but like a flash Bonney's gun was out, covering him. And the chilled-steel grin slicking back the Kid's lips was jarring as a preacher's curse.

Girt yawned back white as ash, the match shaking loose of his fingers. In that brittle hush it seemed as though every owlhooter in the pocket must hear the banging of his heart.

"Come again," Bonney breathed with his gun muzzle bucking Girt's stomach.

But Girt stood sullen, jaws tight locked, his morose glare hard shoved against a yonder peak. And slowly, bit by bit, the wild light cooled from Bonney's stare; and Bonney's head with the slow gliding motion of a thoughtful snake swung consideringly from side to side. Seemed kind of like he was finding it hard to get his mind made up. But Girt kept still till Bonney said: "Don't reckon I much blame you, though, now I stop to think it over. Like enough, was I in your boots, I'd make the same tracks you're makin'. Money talks," he growled with an oath, "an' there ain't no gettin' round it."

"You've sure gone off your feed," Girt shrugged. "You're talkin' loco as a Mex'can." He marveled that he had the guts to make such a crack at Bonney; and Bonney seemed to be marveling too. With his hat-rimmed head cocked to one side, his regard of Girt was baffled. "Doggoned if I don't believe the boy means it," he said, startled, and raked Girt with a wondering stare. Then he shook his head and his scowl came back. "Don't make no diff'rence, though; you'll be makin' the stab 'fore you're finished. I got to watch you like the —"

"Come that's the way you feel," cut in Girt shortly, "I reckon I'm wastin' my time round here. So I allow I'll be pullin' out —"

"Not that easy!" contradicted Bonney, spreading a scowl across his cheeks while his eyes squeezed down to glittering slits. "I'd sure enough be loco was I to let you go ramming out of here! How you s'pose I've kep' above ground this long? — not by sendin' runners out to circulate my where-abouts."

"Say!" demanded Girt. "Why don't you call me a slat-sided double-crossin' bustard an' be done with it!" And the look he hurled at Bonney was every bit as hotly arrogant as that young rascal's own. After a couple of seconds the Kid had the grace to blush — at least he came as close to it as he had ever done. But he covered up with a laugh. Sheathing his pistol with a flourish, he clapped Girt on the back with simulated heartiness.

"Good boy!" he said with a chuckle; and showed Torrance County's new lawman a face as merry with laugh wrinkles as ever it had been in the days when they'd frazzled cows' tails for Chisum.

"Cry-minie!" Girt confessed with relief. "You sure did have me sweatin'! By grab, I thought for a minute you meant it!"

"Shucks," the Kid said with his swaggerish shrug. "Nothin' to it. I was jest tryin' you out like I do all the fellas; and I got to admit, boy, you stacked up han'some. Yes, sir!" and he whacked Girt's shoulder again. "You'll do fine — we'll make a man of you yet!"

Girt stiffened as from the brush that ringed the pocket someone snickered. He scowled at Bonney sulkily. Hell of a thing to say to a guy! But though he racked his mind some feverish, Girt could not lay hand to the right kind of lingo to fit such an awkward occasion. His cheeks got hot and a balked kind of fury rode him. "I — er — you — hell's bells!" he cried; but the Kid waved an airy grin at him.

"You take life a heap too serious, boy," he said as though to soothe him. "What you need is more experience;" and Jim French, sauntering up, nodded sagely. "Tell you what," pronounced the Kid magnanimously; "this little chore that's holdin' me here in the rimrocks, why, I'll deal you in on it; I'll let you ride along with us when we larrup in to take care of it!"

"No, thanks," Girt answered sulkily. Mention of Bonney's chore had brought to mind his own task, still unfinished — that sneaking trick of Benson's that had brought Girt back into Lincoln's turmoil; and he felt a twinge of conscience that he should be idling here while Benson and his half-breed understrapper were packing Merrilyn Matheson ever farther into the wilds. Good Lord! What a fool he was to be swapping gas with these owlhooters while the most precious thing he had ever seen lay at the mercy of such a cutthroat ruffian as Yorba Joe Valmora!

As though sensing the conflict inside

Girt, the Kid stepped across and laid a sympathetic hand on his shoulder. "Shucks! Nothin's bad as it looks like, son; unload your grief an' we'll get it ironed out in a jiffy. What's up?"

Girt flushed at the change in young Bonney's voice; was furious to think how easy the inflections of that charmed voice could sway him. Yet sway him they did; and still sulky and considerably resentful of the fellow's power over him, he was nonetheless soon pouring out his story. "There it is," he wound up awkwardly. "You can see what a mess I've made of things!"

"Shucks, that ain't no mess at all," said Bonney airily. "You ain't never seen no mess, boy! Let's see: Yorba Joe, you said . . . I allow I know that breed. . . ." He screwed his lips up thoughtfully, ran a hand through his curly hair. "Why, sure!" he cried, eyes lighting up. "An' I bet I sabe where he's makin' for —"

"You do!" Girt exclaimed, astounded.

"Wait a sec — lemme think. . . . Seems like he used to fort up in them brakes along the Pecos — Jim!" Bonney turned to where French was hunkered, drawing pictures with a finger in the sand. "Jim — didn't Cash Benson's crowd have a hangout in them hills to the north of South Spring?"

"Chisum's South Spring Ranch?"

"No. I mean Charlie Fritz's place on the Bonito."

Girt didn't see the wink and high-sign the Kid covertly flashed Jim French; but he saw French's whiskered head give a series of short, jerked nods and he leaned forward eyeing him excitedly.

"Why, sure," French mumbled finally, rasping a hand across his jowls. "I believe they did at that, Kid, now you mention it. I'd most near clear forgot it —"

Bonney whirled to Girt triumphantly. "You see? Be jest like rollin' off a log; be a reg'lar lark gettin' this ironed out for you —"

"I don't want to put you to any trouble —"

"Shucks! No trouble, son. Glad to do it for you. We'll take the boys an' drop by an' pay Joe a visit —"

"Say, wait!" Girt eyed the Kid uneasily. "If you take your boys over there, there'll be sure to be a fight —"

"That'll be awful tough," grinned Bonney, "— on Valmora. Might turn out to be what you might call 'the Breed's Las' Stand'."

French pawed his whiskers and guffawed loudly; but Girt didn't see anything to laugh at. If this bunch of owlhooters ever got to throwing lead, the vicinity wasn't going to be a safe place for Clay Matheson's daughter. Not by any jugful!

"That's all right," he said; "I don't give a durn what happens to Valmora — owe him a few on my own hook. But you're forgettin' about that girl —"

"Why, we won't shoot *her* —"

But Girt shook his head. "Not deliberate, probably. But you can't say *who's* goin' to get hit when lead gets to flyin' around." He said uneasily, "I'd be better suited if you could think up some other way to cut it, Kid."

Bonney looked at him keenly. An alive speculation and something else besides was driving bright interest into his glance; and he said, "Sure must be a looker!" and, unaccountably, the conviction in his voice sent a shiver of apprehension up Girt's spinal column.

"Oh — so-so," Girt said, striving to dissemble; and by the feeling of his cheeks guessed Bonney must know him for a liar. "It — er — it ain't that I'm *interested* in her," he floundered, trying to cover up. "Her ol' man is Clay Matheson — the big cattleman and banker. He's the one got me appointed sheriff, you know — got a heap of power an' influence over to Torrance — biggest dog round Broken Stirrup. I wouldn't want him figurin' —"

"Sure, I know," said Bonney smoothly. "You wouldn't be wantin' him to think he'd pinned his tin to a gopher. Playin' in hard luck like you been, he's apt to be thinkin' most *anything* — might even *think* you was in *cahoots* with Yorba Joe an' Cash. We understand. We savvy plenty. But there ain't no need of you frettin'. We'll iron this out as smooth as silk. In fact," he exclaimed, cuffing gloves on thigh, "we'll start for South Spring pronto!"

8

He had ought, Girt supposed, to be down-right overjoyed and thankful that the Kid and his friends were so prompt and open-handedly generous in coming to his aid; it was no small thing, the risk they ran, jogging back into so hostile a country. He should, he guessed, be glad of such aid on *any* terms — and here they were, larruping pell-mell into danger without asking a blessed thing!

It was, perhaps, this very promptness with which the Kid had espoused his cause that was most bothering young Girt Sasabe. It was, of course, the sheer knight-errantry of the thing that had so swiftly stirred Bonney's enthusiasm. Just the same, Broken Stirrup's new sheriff was far from feeling at ease as he rode in that owlhoot company. Now he'd time to think it over, he'd just as lief be riding to this rendezvous with no other company but his Greener. He wished, by grab, he'd had the wit to keep his troubles to himself!

One thing was sure as taxes — any venture in which Bill Bonney had a part was going to be led by Bill Bonney!

And stubborn — Cry-*minie!* You might as well try to move a mountain as to argue with Antrim's stepson! The Kid had a way about him; and when he didn't get it, watch out for the sparks to fly!

Girt had declined the Kid's offer, and thanked him handsomely to boot. But do you think Bill Bonney would listen? Well, not so you could notice it! "I reckon I can make out to handle this. Just tell me where-at's this hangout?" But Bonney had only grinned. "But, dang it," Girt said; "what if you should run into Peppin's posse?"

"Be kind of hard — on Peppin," the Kid chuckled, and French had guffawed roundly.

"But look," Girt implored; "consider my side for a second. Suppose we get tangled with Peppin or Dolan's bunch. Why, hell's fire! What would they think, seein' me, the sheriff of Torrance County, ridin' —"

"You could always say," laughed the Kid, "that we'd captured you."

That had held Girt through the mounting — through the mounting and several miles after. He had ridden morosely in silence; eyes clouded, cheeks twisted and dour. He had pawed up his brains like a dog hunting a bone; seeking some argument that might sway them — that would let him pull the rescue stunt solo. And at last he thought he'd found one.

"Hold up a sec!" he'd cried suddenly. "This ain't goin' to work none whatever! What'll Merrilyn say when she gets back home to her father?"

"She'll say: 'You did a fine stroke of business, Paw, hangin' your tin on Girt Sasabe' —"

"No sir," Girt said doggedly. "What she'll say is, 'Girt Sasabe got me loose all right — but it was Billy the Kid really done it!' "

"Well, don't tell her," the Kid said, grinning. He looked Girt over shrewdly; reknotted his scarf with a smile. Then his long, bony face got serious and a warning crept into his eyes. "You need help cuttin' this trick, Sasabe. Broken Stirrup may have made you a tinbadge, but over here you're some shy on experience. You need me in this business; I know the lay, the hideout and everything. I know this breed, Valmora — what's more, I savvy how to handle him. You don't; an' bein' we're friends, I don't mind helpin' you — fact is, I consider it a privilege. Say no more about it. You're too good a kid to buck out with that breed's knife between your ribs."

Bonney's talk left Girt feeling mean and meeching, without an argument left in the box. He scowled down at his saddle horn and spent the next five miles wishing he'd somebody's hound to kick. Granting all the Kid said was true, that made it no pleasanter to contemplate. And that crack about inexperience rankled like a cockle burr under the blanket. Maybe he *was* inexperienced, but the Kid hadn't no call to throw it up to him. Lack of experience was a thing easily remedied — time would take care of that nicely. In fact, he thought glumly, this jaunt with Bonney would be like to give him all he'd want in a lifetime.

And Merrilyn! What would *she* say when they got back to Broken Stirrup? And there was Colonel Dudley to think about, also. And Cash Benson and that sergeant; and Clay Matheson after he'd talked with his daughter. Girt didn't need the help of any oracle to see that a day of reckoning was coming!

He tried to think what he could have done different — how the things he *had* done had come to bring him to such pass. But regrets, he knew, oiled no sixguns; and there were the Kid's bossy ways to consider.

As sheriff, he ought to be leading this. But he could see right now that if any leading were required, the Kid would damned well supply it! He thought of cutting loose of them, but there again found himself confronted by the Kid's superior policy. Everywhere he turned, young Bonney was there ahead of him — that was the way the Kid was: a mile ahead of things always. Only the Kid had the key to Valmora's whereabouts; and he sure wasn't scattering the knowledge.

Eyeing the Kid's wiry figure where it so jauntily rode up ahead, Girt thought to detect a smug complacency in the arch of that snake-muscled back — thought to read a sly kind of humor into the cant of that leonine head. And he thought bitterly that if he had one ounce of gumption he'd be telling the cocky rooster where the hell to head in at!

Which was all very well to think about, but a heap liable to be something else entirely were a fellow so unconsidering as to put such a notion to words. There was a kind of deterring something in the blue of the young devil's eyes and — well, folks just plain didn't talk that way to Billy-Kid.

Not if they craved to go on breathing.

So Girt, in a lather of complex emotions, scowled down his nose and continued a part of that owlhoot company, sourly cogitating what a hell of a pass it was the law should come to be so helpless.

It was getting on toward the shank of the afternoon when Bonney put a hand up and the company pulled to a halt. "Gettin' kind of close now," Bonney said, squinting. "Want to ride spry an' keep your limpin' blinkers peeled case that so-an'-so gets the wind up. He might not reco'nize me first off an' get to unloadin' some .45-90's; an' I don't want none of you boys gettin' hurt. Girt, you come ahead with me, an' the rest of you vinegarroons fan out some case he tries to run for it. The cache is in that pear tangle —" and he pointed off toward the footslopes where the Mescaleros' ponies were in the habit of getting their drinks. The ground was crisscrossed with the tracks of them; and Girt, fighting back his weariness, wondered alarmedly if by any chance they'd got Merrilyn.

Bonney, with that rapier-keen quick look of his, seemed to divine what had paled up his cheeks so. He said with a thin little grin: "Needn't worry, boy; them Injuns ain't crossin' Cash Benson — he's the guy totes the fire-water for 'em." And then he said reflectively, "She sure must be some looker!" and Girt scowled across at him darkly.

Bonney chuckled. "You rile a sight too easy, boy. Rilin's what gets guys planted — used to have the fault myself till I got hep where 'twas bound to lead me. The fella that lasts in this country, Girt, is the gent that can hold his temper. A man's nerves don't work with his druthers when he's starin' through a red fog of anger."

But Girt sat his saddle lumpish-like, with his look like a face hacked from mesquite. And after a moment, with a shrug Bonney said, "Let's git at it," and led off toward the prickly-pear jungle.

And when they'd come well into it he saw the roof of a clever-hid cabin and marveled that a thing so bulky — though it had but one room — could be concealed by these spiked green pancakes.

Bonney said, "We'll get down now," and swung from the saddle. Girt gingerly followed suit. The Kid, with a quick look roundabout, muttered that he guessed the boys were ready. But, just as Girt was getting a rein on his nervousness and wondering if the Kid were going to stride right up to the door, Bonney, stooping sideways, said:

"Reckon we better make this legal? Want to keep things straight for the record."

Girt's cheeks took color and he fidgeted uneasily. He was picking over his mind for the proper answer when Bonney with a grimace muttered: "Sure, I savvy, boy — you can't well make a deppity of a guy with a price on his noggin." He had learned that word from Tunstall and was proud of it; though his manner reflected no pride just then — only a sort of bewildered dismay that he could not be treated as other men. "You're wantin' to make a hit with the filly, I guess, so — go ahead, make your play an' I'll back it."

That was like him, Girt thought guiltily — generous to a fault. Made him kind of ashamed of the hard thoughts of Bonney he'd been harboring. The Kid was pure gold — no getting around it.

He pulled the old Greener from beneath his stirrup. He could use a pistol; but not in a class with the Kid; and he guessed Valmora, too, could beat him. But a Greener made all men equal; and with the shotgun in a white clamped grip and his heart thumping his chest like a post-driver, he took the lead and started for the door of Benson's shack. Reached out and jerked it open.

The breed was in there. He was crouched beyond the table with his lips drawn back like a wolf. A cocked pistol leered from one hand; there was the glint of a blade in the other.

Girt didn't look for the girl right then; it was no time for picking daisies. "Throw up your hands!" he growled in a thick, choked voice; and felt the Kid's breath fanning his shoulder. It pulsed raw courage into him; and arrogantly, after the manner of the Kid himself, he drawled: "Git 'em up, you slat-sided Injun!"

And lo! — Valmora's hands, suddenly shaking, rose . . . crept up to a level with the beaded headband that bound his lank black hair. And his snaky eyes went wide; fright rimmed the white that showed clear around their pupils. He took a half step back like death had reached out for his windpipe; and Girt, reassured, raked a quick squint round the room — *and found her!* She was there — Clay Matheson's daughter — white and desperate, she was lashed to a pine-slat bunk that was heaped with foul-smelling blankets.

Girt would have jumped at once to unloose her; but the Kid was there already, bending over her, clucking and fussing, while with his slim efficient fingers he was fumbling her cruel bonds. And she — Girt cursed in a passion. She was gazing up at Bonney like he was the last damn Adam, with her star-eyes bright as sapphires and her lips half parted in a look of adoration that well nigh made Girt sick.

His insides boiled to see them so — to see how Bonney had beat him. But that was the Kid's way; a jump ahead of things always, always making each littlest chance count.

Girt gnashed his teeth and scowled at the breed in a fury. "Get shucked of them weapons!" he snarled, so mad he plumb forgot what a scorpion the fellow was. But Valmora made haste to obey. Yet even while his dropped arsenal was sending clatter from the floor, the breed was sneering at Girt, his black eyes mocking, hateful.

The Kid, having chafed some circulation once again into Merrilyn's limbs, now tenderly helped her up and across the room toward Girt. It was like she was in a trance, Girt thought; like she'd hit her head or something. "This here," Bonney told her with a grin, "is Sheriff Sasabe — your dad's new tinbadge. An up-an'-comer from who laid the chunk! Hung on your trail night an' day he did — expect that's how come him to be lookin' so fearful daunsy."

"Oh, how can I ever thank you?" Merrilyn's throaty tones were warm and intimate, suggestive in their hint of love and promise. But Girt Sasabe cursed — for she was still staring up at Bill Bonney!

The Kid patted her hand; held it as though lost in thought for a moment. "Shucks," he spoke at last, reluctantly, "don't thank me — the fellow to thank is the sheriff."

"Yes — yes, I *do* thank him. From the bottom of my heart," sighed Merrilyn; but all the while she was looking sheep's eyes at Bonney.

With a disgusted glower Girt kicked the breed's weapons out of the way, crossed over and plopped down on the bunk. You could have sold him for a postage stamp. "Just like a dadburned woman!" he told himself. "Gone fer Bonney like a ton of flour!" What the hell was the use of being honest?

He slammed up in a moment, stamped across to the door; but opening it, he growled to Bonney: "Tie him up, Bill, will you?" and without bothering to wait for an answer shoved out, letting the door bang shut behind him. He hoped it shook their teeth loose!

At any rate, it appeared to have broken the spell, for a second later Merrilyn came swishing out after him, all breathless and apologetic and bubbling over with praise. "It was so devastatingly good of you — so *heroic!*" she cried, "to risk your life that way for a perfect stranger!" She caught his arm with a pretty gesture. "We won't be strangers long, though, will we?" And she laughed up at him, excitingly, like they shared some delicate secret; and Girt, his pique forgotten, felt his cheeks flush hot with pleasure.

Then the Kid came from the cabin shoving a triced Valmora ahead of him; and though Bonney's eyes were smiling and his lips still wore a grin, Yorba Joe's eyes were round with fright and his face was twisted — ghastly.

"What shall I do with this chipmunk, boss? You fixin' to hang 'im now or later?"

"Oh!" Merrilyn's grip on Girt's arm constricted suddenly. "Surely you won't go so far?" she pleaded. "Because, look — the fellow was only a tool — it is Benson — Cash Benson, that deserves the hanging. This is *his* work — this poor, befuddled Indian is only his creature — his servant. Don't you see it?" she cried, peering up at him.

But just as Girt would have spoken, would have pretended she had swayed him into putting off the breed's execution, Bonney said impatiently: "Make up your mind, boss, one way or the other. Posse'll be gettin' hungry, hangin' round out there in the chaparral —"

"Gosh, yes!" Girt said; "so they will — so they will. S'pose you take a ride out there an' tell 'em I said to come in? Go on," he urged, and grinned just a little, maliciously, at the scowl rocking Bonney's long face.

But could he have foreseen what was to come of sending the Kid out that way, he would have cut off his right arm at the shoulder ere ever he'd spoken the words.

But when the Kid came back the mischief was done. Girt had found the girl's horse and saddled it. Helping her up, he looked around and found he could contemplate the Kid for once with something like satisfaction. "Were they hungry?" he called facetiously.

But Bonney's face stayed grave. "They was gone," he told Girt dryly. "They've cleared out on us, lock, stock and barrel!"

9

"Gone?" Girt echoed blankly. "Mean to say them birds have run out on us?"

"If they ain't, it'll take some provin'," Bonney said grimly. "There ain't a swivel-jawed one in sight an' their sign is a half hour old —"

"But what the hell!" Girt growled in bafflement. "What would they want to pull out for?"

What indeed! Had Girt the answer to that one he'd have done a lot of things different in future. But if the Kid knew he wasn't telling; he just shrugged his slim shoulders and spat: "Takin' 'em by an' large," he observed, "I'd say sheriffs' posses was considerable unreliable. Man that puts any faith in 'em is sure leanin' on a broken reed." He looked Girt over surly, just as if his owlhooter outfit had really been a posse that had cut its stick and run. Cuffing some of the dust from his clothing, he stared up at Girt inquiringly. "Well?" he said. "What's the order now? We goin' to

105

camp here an' chance them Injuns, or was you figgerin' on linin' straight out fer the Capitans as bein' the shortest cut for Torrance?"

That word "Injuns" worked on Girt like liniment on a balky horse — as Bonney likely figured it would.

Girt took a quick scowl around uneasily. He could not fail to observe how rapidly the evening was sliding away toward dusk, nor how much longer than they had been were the sun's bent shadows that were wiring the range with somber patterns.

"I reckon," Girt muttered, "we had better strike for them mountains. Mebbe," he said hopefully, "we'll catch up with some of your — with that dad-burned bunch-quittin' posse."

"Mebbe," Bonney said, and turned away with a sly little smile.

Night settled down black — as black as a dead steer's gizzard. Lowering, grim, portentous, a narrow reef of cloud extended across the sky's pit-blackness like a harbinger of evil; and what few stars dared show their faces flickered feeble as a guttering lantern.

They had covered ten miles when Bonney said thoughtful-like: "Don't you reckon, boy, we better pull up an' bed down around here someplace? That girl looks pretty gaunted — see how she slumps in the saddle? I allow she's weary as a dog-chased coyote an' is prob'ly dyin' for a rest."

It was, Girt thought, just like the Kid to be always thinking of others. And he was grateful, too, for the softness of tone with which Bonney had put the suggestion. They were riding stirrup to stirrup, with the girl and Valmora hitting it up some couple of horse-lengths ahead. But he said dubiously: "What about them damn redskins?"

Bonney shrugged. "Have to chance 'em, I reckon. Anyways, it's been my experience they much prefer God's daylight for the pullin' of their didoes. An' we're a little off their path here — they don't often ride this far northward. Unless they're off their trail a heap, they'll never even notice us. That girl sure looks dog-tired."

So after pondering the advice a spell, Girt decided to take it. After all, refreshed by a good night's rest, they would make better time tomorrow. So he called a halt; and they all climbed down from their horses.

Girt arranged the girl's blankets — even

gave her his own and Valmora's, while the
Kid took care of the horses and saw to the
prisoner's rawhides. He built a tiny fire in
the shelter of two big boulders and was
hunkering down with the makings when
Bonney came dragging some branches.
"Thought mebbe," he said, "I better fix
some kind of shelter for the lady. The dew
is pretty fierce in these parts sometimes an'
you wouldn't want her to be takin' cold, I
reckon."

He didn't shout it, but he managed to
make it loud enough for Merrilyn to hear;
and while Girt, stiff-cheeked and scowling,
was still trying to decide if this stunt of the
Kid's was deliberate, Bonney got to work
and in two shakes had a little ramada fixed
up a few feet from the fire; its floor carefully sheathed with spruce branches. He
brought his blanket for a bed sheet and,
helping Merrilyn over, draped Girt's and
Valmora's blankets round her with a smile.
"I reckon you ought to sleep good now,
ma'am. Just relax; there won't nothin'
bother you. The sheriff an' I'll stand
guard."

There was nothing Girt could say without the girl hearing, so he kept his notions
to himself. But that they were hardly boon
companions was evidenced by the way he

kept smoke boiling from the pipe the Kid had given him.

Hunkered across the fire from him, the Kid rolled endless cigarettes and puffed them one right after the other; not furious, the way Girt smoked, but thoughtfully appreciative, like a man who lived much alone. And his eyes were thoughtful, moody, as he stared down into the coals. But he finally rose when it seemed like Merrilyn was sleeping and, catching Girt's eye, said quietly: "Keep your eyes skinned now; I'm goin' to snatch me a little shut-eye. You take this first watch, boy, an' I'll take on for the graveyard shift — keep awake now!" And off he went into the shadows before Girt could rake up a protest.

Girt glowered at the fire resentfully. The Kid was too damn free with his orders. Telling that girl he was goin' to stand guard and then soon's she'd got her eyes closed taking himself off for a snooze! He sure had a gall, by grab! "I'll take the graveyard shift!" he'd said. Girt had a notion not to call him; but after a bit he changed his mind. That would suit the Kid down to the ground, like enough. "To hell with him!" Girt grunted sourly.

But after a while, when the fire burned

low and his chin got to digging his chest, a deal of Girt's anger abated. After all, taken by and large, the Kid was a pretty good friend; it wasn't every saddle-pounder would take his crowd and slam pell-mell into danger just to help a guy out with his problems! If the Kid wanted to put on a few little airs — why, after all, he'd earned them. It was just the Kid's natural thoughtfulness that made him attentive to Merrilyn. He didn't mean nothing by it — wasn't trying to grab off Girt's girl.

Sure was a dang cold night, Girt thought; and black as a black cat's overcoat. The fire felt good and he thought kind of vague-like of building it up; but settled back more comfortably against his warm rock instead. The wind moaned through the spruce and dwarf cedars and whirled stray sparks from the campfire. The smell of the smoke was soothing and the fire's warmth made him drowsy and he quite forgot the eeriness of this place and the Mescaleros' proximity. A coyote barked away off in the brush; and a wolf's defiance came drifting from a hilltop and that was the last thing he was conscious of till he jerked bolt upright with the sound of a shot in his ears.

False dawn's grayness paled the sky and

peopled the range with dim shadows, and it was on one of these that Girt's alarmed eyes were fastened as the echoes fell off the rimrocks. The shadow moved, became the crouched figure of a man. Girt grabbed out his gun and was cocking the hammer when the Kid's calm voice said quietly: "Take it easy, son — no call to get the wind up. I jest been pottin' a coyote."

"A coyote!" Girt said; and Merrilyn sprang up with a cry.

Bonney, head canted, stood eyeing them while he punched the spent shell from his shotgun. "Now, ma'am," he soothed, "you jest rest quiet. There ain't nothin' goin' to hurt you — not while I'm around. Depend on it."

Girt put his gun up with a scowl and stood peering around trying to locate Valmora. But the halfbreed wasn't where they'd left him, and with an oath Girt grabbed up his Greener and —

"Where you goin', Sheriff?" Bonney's tone was curious.

"That dang breed —"

"Shucks! I got him, didn't I? Thought he was pretty slick, I reckon, crawlin' over here with that bowie knife — but I fixed his hash all right, you bet! You won't need to boil *him* any coffee." He stared at the girl sympathetically, put a hand on her shivering shoulder. "There, there, now, ma'am; don't take on so hard about it. He can't bother you any now — not even if he *was* within a ace of liftin' your pretty hair —"

"*What?*" cried Girt with a strangled oath.

But the Kid just shrugged his slim-shouldered shrug. "There he is," he said. "Go take a look."

And sure enough! The breed's sprawled form lay not three feet from where the girl had been sleeping. Face down with one knee half doubled and an arm twisted under him and a knife glinting dully in the fist of the arm stretched before him.

It certainly looked to be just like young Bonney had said; and Girt shuddered for thought of what his sleeping might have let happen to Merrilyn. Then a thought clicked over at the back of his head and he said to Bonney: "I thought you tied —"

"I reckoned so, too; but I guess I didn't tie him tight as I aimed to. That's the trouble with these breeds — slipp'rier 'n slobbers. If it comes to that, though," Bonney said tartly, "I thought you was goin' to keep your eyes skinned. When a fellow stands guard seems like he'd ort to keep awake." He scowled at Sasabe grimly. "Lucky I'm a mighty light sleeper."

And Girt hung his head in shame; and could not find it in his heart to rightly blame the girl for the look she gave Bill Bonney. He had saved her life and Girt's life, too; he had proved himself a hero.

It was in a pretty meeching frame of mind that Girt tramped off for the horses. You could sell him for a postage stamp — a hell of a sheriff he was!

10

He was still feeling about as useful as a .22 cartridge in an eight-gauge shotgun when, some ten or twelve minutes later, he returned to the camp site leading their saddled broncs. "Expect we better hit the trail," he mentioned gruffly.

His impression of being rather an unnecessary third in this trio kept his eyes upon the pommel as he said it. It certainly wasn't his day of the month to shine; and the glintery star he'd last night pinned back on his vest made him in the light of the Kid's recent exploit feel pretty cheap. But when young Bonney in his patronizing drawl said airily: " 'Fraid I got to disagree with you again, boy," Girt's mind began to function.

"What's that?" he said.

As though in intimate conversation, they had been standing close together, the Kid and Clay Matheson's daughter. But now Bonney drew away a little and his smile held an edge of mockery as he surveyed

Girt with an easy tolerance.

"It would be plumb foolish," he remarked, "to set out for Torrance in daylight. I been thinkin' it over an' I tell you, son, these Injuns is gettin' plain wicked. Best thing we can do is to stick where we are until nightfall — an' jest as well anyhow; these horses can do with more rest. So," he added, "can Merrilyn," and he looked at the girl with a grin.

So it was "Merrilyn" now, Girt thought with an oath. The Kid was sure a quick worker. Broken Stirrup's young sheriff looked him over more critical than had been his habit in the past. What was it, he wondered, that so endowed Bonney with luck? What had the man that other men lacked? Was it the size of his guts made the difference?

There was nothing especially imposing in either the Kid's look or his build. An old slouch hat that bent his big ears was jauntily clapped on his head; and beneath this the gleam of flaxen curls spread a sheen of pale gold to his neckerchief. He'd a long bold nose that sat not quite straight on a face that was too long and horsy. The wide, awry mouth in the grin below showed teeth that were horsy also. Nor in this land of big-boned men was the slight stature of his snake-hipped figure impressive; in another it would have been called what it was — plain runty.

But no one called Bill Bonney that — leastways not where he could hear them. Despite his shortcomings and physical defects, there was about him an unget-aroundable air — a something that caused men to pause and think twice before doing any laughing around him.

It wasn't his garb that checked them. He wore a slack and sloppy range rider's coat and a vest that always hung open; and under the vest like a suspension-bridge cable swung the wide bright links of a great gold chain that was draped across his shirtfront and fastened to the English hunting watch that Tunstall once had given him — or so he said. A broad belt rode his right hip slanchways and dropped away to the open scuffed pouch that on his left thigh packed a sixgun; and rough, baby trousers were carelessly jammed into fancy-topped, run-over range boots. And under the stirrup fenders of the saddled bronc Girt held was his nickel-barreled, high-powered rifle.

Yet it was neither this gun nor his pistol, Girt thought, that mostly folks seemed to be scared of. No more was it the man himself that made all comers step easy. It was the rep he had built in these last few months that earned the Kid his wide berth.

That — and the look that could stare from his eyes. Chilled steel was plumb hot by comparison.

Having heard the Kid's speech and eyeing him as he stood now, poised a half step or so before Merrilyn, an ugly thought ran through young Girt's mind. He tried to dismiss the notion as unworthy. But it proved stronger than his will to deny it.

Could the Kid, he wondered, have killed that breed deliberate and some way rigged things up to look the way they did look? It might have been, a voice hinted, that Bonney had no wish to find his style cramped by lugging around any prisoner. And — yes, by grab! It *did* look funny the way the Kid's men had beat it!

About as funny as a crutch.

Girt swore at himself and refused in a fury to follow such thought any further. Billy wasn't like that. He was staunch and loyal as the day was long; open-handed to a fault — always thoughtfully considerate of a friend. To have killed the breed that way and for such reason would have been a scurvy cur trick — not at all in keeping with the Kid's known character. Sure, the

Kid rustled a few steers now and then, but — hell! who didn't? One thing Girt was sure of: If Bonney had aimed to kill Vamora, no matter what his private reason, he never in the world would have done it that way. He'd have forced the breed to draw; would have given him a fighting chance.

Perhaps he had, suspicion whispered. . . . Or as much of a chance as any man had who was made to match draws with Bill Bonney.

Girt cursed himself proper — railed at such notions; called himself seven kinds of jackass. But the damage was done. The seed was planted, was rooted beyond all protest. Never again, he thought, would things be quite the same between them; never again would they quite recapture the old free and easy ways. Henceforward there must ever be some faint edge of restraint to their relations, some reserved or cautious watchfulness. Some need for a care and attention — though Girt swore this shouldn't be so.

As though sensing in that uncanny way of his something of what was romping through Girt's mind, young Bonney chuckled. "We'll get along," he said. "There's things can come between some fellas can bust their friendship all to flinders; but me an' you is diff'rent, Girt. We got a little savvy. The old crowd's all split up now. 'F you was to pasear out to the Fence Rail you'd find a new string runnin' the bullpen; the old crowd all is gone. Some —" In the pause a shadow crossed his cheeks; his lips took on a kind of tightness. "Some is dead, some pulled out, the most of 'em scattered to hell-an'-gone. Here's you with tin pinned on your vest an' me with my mug all over the trees an' telegraph poles. But a friend's a friend for all of that, an' a real friend, boy, never changes."

The old whimsical grin chased the soberness off his face then; and he yawned and stretched and fetched out the makings. "It's sure a queer world, boy, an' no guy can guess what the morrow's goin' to bring him. But one chance — one chance in a million is all I ask," and he licked his cigarette with a laugh. "Go peel the gear from them horses, Girt, an' put 'em on close hobbles. We'll be wantin' 'em, come evenin' —"

"I vote we do our ridin' now," Girt said, "an' —"

"You're overruled then, Tinbadge. Not safe."

"But you said," Girt objected, "that —"

"I know." Bonney waved a hand at him. "But I've jest recollected somethin'. That new buck makin' medicine for the Mescaleros has been workin' up quite a followin' — 'special 'mongst the feather-wanters. Been tellin' 'em if they can get 'em a pale-face squaw with dove gray eyes they can waltz right off the reservation. An' if it happens they can pick up a squaw with gray eyes *an'*" — he shot a meaningful look at Merrilyn — "*gold hair*, then, boy, they'll really have somethin'! Now, chances are they wouldn't ketch us, but — do you want to take the risk?"

And Girt saw then that he couldn't; not after the Kid put it that way. So he glumly pulled the gear from the broncs and turned them out on hobbles. And when he came back the breed's corpse was gone and Bonney was talking with Merrilyn. Something about "art and literachoor"; he wasn't in no mood to listen. Grabbing up his Greener, he stomped off up the draw until he found his way up to the rimrocks; and sat there with his cheeks gone dour, gazing bitterly off into distance. Grant him the best of intentions, there was no getting around the fact that Bill Bonney was hell with the women. They hadn't any victuals with them, but if they had it sure would have spoilt Girt's dinner the way that fool girl played up to him.

"Just a dadburned flirt!" was his verdict, but that was no kind of balm for Girt's ailment.

The sun was gilding earth's canvas with a new day's splendor when Girt with the girl and Bonney rode into the owlhooters' rendezvous. The whole crew was there and the cold crisp air of the sparkly morning was pleasantly tanged with cookery as they stiffly climbed down from their saddles. The girl's face was drawn with fatigue and the trip hadn't rested Girt none; but the Kid's merry eyes were more twinkling than ever and he seemed in the highest of spirits. Even the lecture he gave his men for their desertion of the sheriff was more in the nature of a blessing than a rawhiding; and Girt thought resentfully that everyone but himself seemed to consider the whole thing a lark. But he had the wisdom to keep that opinion to himself; and when the Kid grabbed up a tin plate and went and scrubbed it in the spring before smilingly handing it to Merrilyn with the advice to "Pitch in an' help yourself, ma'am," he managed to keep his mouth shut also. But deep inside his soul he seethed. A one-eyed jaster with both hands tied could see how the girl went for Bonney! He was the brass-collar dog round her all right; and Girt gulped his grub in a fury.

All day he juned around doing nothing, consumed with an impatience to be gone. He watched the owlhooters try their luck with cards, sprawled around like Apaches on their saddle blankets. He even permitted himself to be coaxed into a game of stud-horse poker, and was so indifferent to his surprising success as to lose the whole works on the single brash turn of a card. So marked was his indifference, the whole crew looked after him with an unveiled curiosity when he finally turned away. Till Scurlock with a broad wink sent a glance toward where in the shade of a mesquite's tangle the Kid sat chinning with Merrilyn. Then the whole crew grinned and French guffawed.

But if Sasabe heard them he gave no sign; nor did he join the girl and Bill Bonney. He'd tried that once and had no further desire to augment the rapt audience to the Kid's discourse on the classics. It made him plumb sick the way Merrilyn sat and gulped down all that stuff like 'twas gospel.

The Kid had allowed he thought it might be safe for them to start for Broken Stirrup after night fell; but when night wore round he took Girt aside. "Look here," he said gravely, "I don't know's you'd be doin' right to pull out of here just yet. Better stick around another day or two just in case. Bowdre says Benson's been prowlin' around Lincoln with blood in his eye — says he's been askin' about you —"

"Hell with him!" Girt said shortly. "If he knows what's good, he'll keep outa my way!"

But Bonney just looked at him sadly. "You got any idee how fast that buck is with a gun, boy? Well, I'm here to say his draw shames lightnin' by comparison. He's so fast — well, I'll say frank I don't know if I could beat him myself. Cool off a bit an' think this over. I know you're in a lather to get back to Broken Stirrup, but where the hell would Miz' Matheson be was Benson to cross your track and down you? Shucks, a guy like Benson — you can't tell, boy. He's liable to lay up some place in the rimrocks an' pot you without a chance!"

Girt knew that was so; and the fact did little to improve his temper. What he wanted now was to get out of here. But the Kid had an eye to his safety. "Tell you what," Bonney said. "You stick around a couple days an' I'll have one of the boys tool Benson off on a goose chase. It'll be a —"

Girt said weakly: "What the hell kind of a sheriff —"

"What kind of a sheriff'll you be *dead*, boy? Now look —" The Kid tapped him on the chest, eyed him earnestly. "A lawman's first duty is the public safety. Which bein' the case, where would Merrilyn be was Benson to blow a window through your skull, eh? Why, she'd be worse off than ever!"

"If you think she ain't safe with me," Girt came back, "suppose you ride along with us. Bring your gang if you like —"

"Can't be did." The Kid shook his head. "You're forgettin' my business in Lincoln."

"Ride in tonight then —"

"Uh-uh. Time ain't turned quite ripe yet. Be another couple days before —"

"I'll be sayin' so long then," Girt told him.

Bonney eyed him quietly, intent-like.

Girt flushed; abruptly scowled with annoyance.

"I thought you was a friend of mine." The Kid said it soft — kind of wistful; and Girt scowled down at his boots. "Seems like a friend," the Kid went on, "ought to be willin' to take some advice. Of course, if you want to be bull-headed an' pull out plumb regardless, I got no way of stoppin' you, but . . ."

"Well," Girt grumbled, "I'll wait until mornin' —"

"You're showin' good sense," said Bonney heartily and, clapping Girt approvingly on the shoulder, arm in arm led him back to the fire.

But morning brought round a new problem. Some of the horses — Girt's and Merrilyn's among them — kept in the draw beyond the tunnel, were missing. It was thought at first they had wandered off in search of better grazing. But when Bonney, scowling, with Girt and French and Charlie Bowdre, rode out to have a look, truth painted a graver picture. The Kid's oath and wildly beckoning arm brought them piling into the mesquite. "Lookit that!" Bill Bonney cried, pointing. And — "Injuns, by God!" breathed Jim French.

Girt stared with a shiver. Moccasin sign was plain.

And plain seemed to be the story. During the night the wily Mescaleros had pulled a slick raid and gone off with near all the Kid's horses. Only the four they were now astride of had been saved them by someone's forethought in bringing them into the pocket.

The Kid's face was a study; and Jim French — like he was conducting a course in profanity — was making it very plain about what should be done with redskins down to the last copper-faced papoose. But that was not getting their horses back and Girt, himself boiling at this new prospective delay to departure, was all for going after the Mescaleros hotfooted.

But Bowdre counseled waiting. "Let's not split our pants out now. Them bucks around here," he said, "has pretty generally been friendly with us fellas. I'd say this was young bucks' work — that the old heads wasn't in on it. An' if that's so, we'll be gettin' them horses back; or anyways a proposition before —"

"I'll 'proposition' 'em!" cried Jim French with an oath. "Jest let me git my hands wrapped round them Injuns' windpipes —"

But the Kid shut him off with a look. He stood there hipshot — Bonney; eyes thoughtful, face considering. "Believe Charlie's right," he said. "We'll wait —"

"What! Pay them bustards fer what

belongs to us!" Jim French growled out in a fury; but again the Kid's look silenced him.

"We'll wait," the Kid repeated.

11

So, leaving Bowdre to watch for a possible messenger from the Mescaleros, Bonney led the way back into the pocket. And the old problem of how to pass time started over again in grim earnest. Girt would have talked over their plight with Merrilyn; but he couldn't well do that before Bonney, and the Kid was always around her. So with a sulky scowl Broken Stirrup's young sheriff went back to playing cards for matchsticks.

Scurlock quit the game after a spell and resaddled one of the four remaining horses. "Reckon I'll take a pasear into town," he allowed. "You fellas wantin' me to fetch you back anything?"

They told him, "Some likker," and he rode off with a laugh. "I should think," Girt remarked, "he would be a mite worried about showin' himself around Lincoln."

"Oh, Doc has friends there," Hendry Brown told him; and it must have been funny, for all the rest of them guffawed.

The Kid looked over to see what was up, grinned mechanically and went back to his toreador pleasures with Merrilyn. He must, Girt thought, have been telling it creepy, for her face was aglow with excitement.

She had on the Kid's jacket now, Girt noticed, scowling. Not that she couldn't use the covering — for the woodpeddler's garb Valmora had made her wear was little better than nothing with its many rents and patches — but Girt had earlier offered his own coat to her and she'd turned it down without compromise.

The card game went on and on like the clatter of Bonney's recitals; lost its aspect of sport and became in its dullness pure drudgery. There was some talk of knocking off for a while for a nooning, but just as Brown picked the cards up for a last desultory shuffle, Charlie Bowdre rode out of the tunnel and slid from his bronc beside Bonney.

Every owlhooter dropped the game, leaned forward with neck craned to listen.

"Want to buy any horses? There's a fella outside wants to sell some."

"What!" said the Kid, and Girt saw his jaw drop. "Who wants —"

"Some Injun," grinned Bowdre. "Didn't

mention his name; but he's got fifteen broncs — five bucks apiece — an' I reckon you better be buyin' 'em." They looked at each other, Bill Bonney and Bowdre; and suddenly Girt Sasabe saw it.

Like a flash he could see what had happened! The Kid had rustled his own horses and someway the redskins had got them; Bonney'd hidden them out so Girt wouldn't be leaving and the Mescaleros had found them. Now the Kid must dig up five bucks apiece or really be out his remuda — and it served him damned right, Girt thought with a curse, for blaming his tricks on the 'Paches!

Girt wheeled up from his place, growled at Bowdre: "Where is this buck? I'll take two of them broncs so golram fast it'll make his eyes spin!"

Bowdre looked at Bonney and the Kid said smoothly, "Just a minute, son; *I* do the buyin' for this crowd." And, excusing himself from Merrilyn with a flourish, he caught Bowdre's horse by the cheekstraps. "Has he got the broncs with him?" And at Charlie's nod the Kid swung into the saddle.

But Girt swung right up behind him. "Let's go!" he said grimly, and kicked the surprised horse in the ribs.

"Well, at least," Bonney said when the horse trade was done with, "you'll not be leaving before grub? Now wait —" he said, raising his hand; "I know you think that was a scurvy trick, an' mebbe it was, now I think of it. But the truth is, boy, I like you. I like the way you stack up, and the way that you handle that Greener —"

"What you like," Girt told him bitterly, "is Merrilyn Matheson. Why lie about it?"

There was a look for a second in the Kid's blue eyes that was like a snake-tail's rattle. Then a cool grin changed the set of his face and Bonney said deprecatingly, "That girl? You think I'm gone on *her?* Shucks, boy, that idee does you no credit. The Pecos hills is full of girls — an' a lot a sight prettier 'n she is; I take 'em where I find 'em an' leave 'em there when I go.

"But with you, Girt," he said, soft, persuasive, "it's diff'rent — a good lad's hard to find these days; I need someone to ride the river with. Those boys," he added, waving a hand toward the tunnel, "is all right after their fashion. But a man can't put no trust in them. Was they to get the chance, they'd knife me faster than Jack-be-quick! I could trust you, boy — I been hopin' you might side me." And he looked at Girt with all the old charm and wistfulness Girt remembered from their cow-punching days at John Chisum's.

Nor was Girt unaware of the compliment Bonney thus paid him. But his appreciation of it was tinged with something no amount of fine flattery could surmount. A month ago — ten days ago, even — Girt would have jumped at this chance Bonney offered. But he had his eyes open now, he told himself grimly; he'd had enough of Billy-Kid's tricks.

"No," he said. "I'm a sheriff now, Bill — I can't do 'er. With all the good will in the world, I got my duty to do and —"

"I see!" Bonney came back at him bitterly. "I ain't good enough for you any more, eh? You're a tinbadge now an' you can't pal around with the snakes!"

Girt's cheeks blushed a protest; he stammered, looked embarrassed. "I never called you a snake — an' it ain't that anyway. It's just —"

"Sure, I know," the Kid told him, scowling. He stared off into the distance a bit. And when he turned back, the old grin smoothed the warped look from his cheekbones. "I been a fool to think you would join me. You can't, of course; so let's say no more about it, boy. But you'll stay for grub-pile, won't you?"

So of course Girt told him "Yes" — there was nothing else he *could* say.

They were halfway through the meal, with Girt in a deal better spirits now that departure at last seemed at hand, when Hawkface — Doc Scurlock — rode in through the tunnel and tossed a neat parcel at Bonney. "There y'are," he said, and went off to put his bronc up.

Bonney pushed the package over to Merrilyn. "Just a little present," he smiled, "in the hope you'll think of me sometimes."

Face flushed with pleasure, Merrilyn stopped eating in an excitement to see what he'd given her. Under her hasty fingers the wrapping fell away to disclose a brand new charro costume, all tricked out with tiny bells and thread of gold and silver, and a big cream sombrero with chin strap and snakeskin band.

Girt, watching, saw the girl, cheeks glowing, throw a rapturous look at Bonney. Her eyes were bright as stars, he thought; and cursed to himself in a passion. Would he never, he wondered bitterly, be shut of Bonney's forethought? Always the Kid got ahead of him; always he grabbed off the honors!

Girt gulped the rest of his food down in

silence and shoved to his feet when the rest started rolling their smokes. About to tell the girl to be ready to leave soon's he'd caught up and saddled their horses, he shut his teeth down hard on the notion. That had ever been his trouble — always going off half cocked! He'd play it different hereafter; he'd take a page from Bill Bonney — he'd play it the smart way, smoothly.

So, saying nothing, he sauntered off with a smile; and paused to pack the pipe Bonney'd given him when he saw Scurlock making over in his direction. He was bringing a light up from his boot-sole just as Hawkface stopped him.

"Say — hold on!" cried Scurlock loudly. "I got some news for you, boy! Did you know there's a reward out for you? Well, there is! Ol' Dudley's put a big one up; says you're goin' to be an example, by God, if you're the last one he ever furnishes! Now what do you think of that?"

"Well, I got to admit it's interesting," Girt said, keeping his poker face. "Quite interesting — if true." And he smiled at Scurlock as the Kid might have smiled, and Hawkface stepped back with an oath.

"Are you doubtin' my word?" he said, ugly.

But Girt only smiled. "I wouldn't think of doubtin' you. What I mean was, I don't allow Dudley can cut it."

The gang pricked up their ears, but Scurlock looked at him and snorted. "Lemme tell you somethin', boy!" he snarled, and shook a finger under Girt's nose. "The colonel's got every road out of Lincoln patrolled — in fact, every road out of these mountains! An' he's told all them mighty troopers that if you don't stop when they holler, they're to give you everything in their barrels!"

"Ho-hum!" Girt yawned elaborately, covering his mouth with a hand. "That's very interesting, I'm sure. Might even worry me a mite was I figurin' to be goin' any place — which I ain't. Long's Miz' Matheson ain't in no lather, I expect I'll stay on here a spell."

And he felt plumb tickled inside him at the look that came over Bill Bonney. It was plain that he'd got the Kid guessing; and Merrilyn looked mystified, too. "Why — why, yes," she stammered, flushing. "I expect we *could* stay a day or two longer . . . though it will fret Daddy something awful. If he ever finds out —"

"Shucks, we could always say," Girt chuckled, "that it took a bit longer to find you. Mebbe the Kid, if he'd put his mind to it, could shine the yarn up even better — how about it, Bill? Couldn't you augur up some big one about how I had to fight forty-odd redskins, not to mention three-four cougars an' a bob-cat, besides Cash Benson's whole gang singlehanded, before I could rescue the lady?"

And it did him good, the baffled looks that came over that whole bunch's faces.

Strangely enough, Bill Bonney, after he'd finished eating, did not go as was his custom and spend the rest of the day with Merrilyn; he did not even go near her. He did not stir at all, but sat beside the grease-wood fire, motionless — save for such brief movements as marked the rolling of innumerable cigarettes, absorbed, a half-frown playing fitfully across his high-boned features. He had the strained, intent look of a man wrestling with a difficult problem; and Girt, content to leave him with it, meandered over to entertain Merrilyn.

But she was not in her happiest mood, it appeared. Not even the pleasure of lolling around in her new man's clothing, nor the bold flirtatious glances her charro suit attracted from the outlaws, seemed able to lift her to the heights of charm she had been languishing on Bonney. Five or six of her short answers proved enough to send Girt back to watch the saddle-blanket gamblers' battle for matchsticks.

But even this palled on him at last. There were only half of them playing, and the game was blackjack, not especially interesting to watch. So finally, thinking this as good a time as any to be getting a little shut-eye, Girt wandered off into the brush on a hunt for a good spot to pound his ear.

It was just as he'd thought to find one that he became aware of the voices. Two words caught at his attention — *Bonney* and *Lincoln*. Without hesitation he slipped up closer and parted the brush to peer through. Being somewhat of a lamb among Philistines, he felt no shame in eavesdropping; and those who hold that people in his position hear nothing of good to themselves were proved a little mistaken. Two men were talking, French and Hendry Brown; and what they said bugged Girt's eyes out.

They were examining a small dark bottle; appeared to be experimenting with its contents. "You reckon the shade'll be right?" Brown asked; and French with a snort said: "What diff'rence? We're pullin' this job at night, ain't we? Who's to see in the dark? Besides, tricked out the way we'll be, if there's doubt of us bein' greasers, why, so much the better; they'll swear we're some of Dolan's bunch — which is just what Billy's wantin'! He's got a real head on 'im, Bonney has! Ain't many would've thought of this stunt; kill two birds with the same stone, easy as rollin' water off a duck's back! Just think! Robbin' that prissy widder an' layin' the blame on Dolan — we'll get a laugh outa this for years!" And French gave Brown a hearty clap on the back and the two of them stood there chuckling.

The sheer audacity of it took Girt's breath away. His heart thumped like a tom-tom till he thought the whole camp would hear it. So this was why the Kid had been hanging so close to Lincoln! This was the "chore" he had to do! They were going to rob McSween's widow and hang up the blame on Jim Dolan!

The scope and magnitude of the project, the Machiavellian cunning of a mind that could dream up such a spiteful, ornery plan, all bore the brand of Bonney's personality. There was no doubting that part! This was just such a thing as the Kid might concoct — he'd always been a hand to love horseplay. And it was just such a thing as would tickle that malign sense of humor he'd been amazing Girt with these last days.

Yet it seemed incredible that even *he* — daring and reckless as Girt knew the Kid to be — would have the gall to invade again the stronghold of an enemy who had just finished thwacking him so proper — the bailiwick of Peppin, who had sworn to have his scalp!

And then Girt saw the logic of it. *One chance in a million* had ever been the Kid's loud boast. And what a chance this present one! The chance at one swift stroke not only of amassing much plunder, but, by the very deed, the chance of sending the man who had out-foxed him down to the inspection of posterity drenched in a reek that would never die! Jim Dolan would never outlive the ignominy of robbing a murdered man's widow!

Girt was jerked from his pondering by the sound of a startled gasp. Whirling, he found himself confronted by Merrilyn Matheson. She stood almost at his shoulder; and while he stared at her — hardly more embarrassed than was the girl herself — he heard the scuff of departing boots and knew that the men had gone.

He was the first to break the silence. "You heard?"

She nodded, white-cheeked, black eyes snapping. He had never seen gray eyes look black as that before; she was hopping mad, he guessed, and supposed her anger to be directed against himself for over-hearing French's conversation.

But he was wrong; her anger was for Bonney, as he discovered a moment later. Dissembling, not knowing how much she'd heard and hoping she hadn't heard Bonney's name mentioned, he said: "Wisht I knew which Mexicans it was that was figurin' to rob McSween's widow —"

The scorn of her glance choked him. "You can save your breath, Mister Sasabe; I wasn't born yesterday! You know well as I do, every Mexican step has a Texican step behind it! No Mexican pulls a stunt like that of his own choosing — *Mexicans!* You heard what those men said! It's this fine Bill Bonney you've been playing up to that's planning to rob McSween's widow!"

Girt just stared at her, pop-eyed.

"Now what have *I* done," he finally floundered, "to deserve —"

"Done!" she cried. "That's just the trouble — you haven't done *anything* — and never will. You haven't sense enough to get in out of the rain! Here I've been playing that braggart ruffian along for the last two days just to help you — just to give you a *chance* to do something! You make me sick! Get away! Don't touch me! A fine sheriff *you* turned out to be! Just wait till I talk to my dad!"

Girt fell back a step under that fury. Her contempt was like a lash, each stroke cutting him to the bone.

But when she opened her mouth to resume, he cried: "Hey! Wait a minute now! Gimme a chance —"

"Chance!" She laughed at him. "How many chances you need — *boy!*" And her laugh came again, mocking, brittle. "Why, you haven't the nerve to cross up a man like Bill Bonney — you haven't the nerve of a *jackrabbit!*"

Girt, red-cheeked and furious, made a violent gesture. With an oath he slammed round to quit her — and stopped, like a bullet had clutched him. Ten feet away, with his hands on his hips, stood Billy the Kid, grim and mocking.

12

"Your pardon if I'm intrudin' on a private conversation," the Kid drawled suavely; and you could see the devils dancing in his eyes. "I just stopped by to ask, Girt, if you're sure-enough aimin' to stay for a spell or if you're figurin' to pull out come night?"

There was a chance here, handed him on a platter, but Girt's emotions were too involved at the moment for him to do any very clear thinking. Nor was the look of Bonney's gray eyes at all helpful. Girt shifted his weight uneasily, flushed and looked foolish and scowled.

But the Kid seemed to understand. He chuckled and looked so knowing, it was all Girt could do to hold still. A past master at rawhiding was Bonney. He said with a smirk, "Guess I better talk to you later — didn't know you was playin' the bear. My apologies, ma'am!" He bowed low, shucking his hat with a flourish.

Then the girl found her voice. "Bear! Would you call that weasel a *bear?*" And she tossed her head with a scorn that left Girt wilted.

"Well, shucks —" the Kid said; but Merrilyn wheeled and flounced off toward the fire in a huff. And the Kid, still chuckling, with a final look at Girt sauntered after her.

Red-faced and mightily discomforted, Girt stared after them glumly. But not for long. That final look of Bonney's jerked him back to the issues pronto; a sly, designing look it had been, and glinting like bright sun on steel.

What had the Kid got up his sleeve? What had that look portended? That Bonney had heard sufficient to know his plans for Lincoln had been uncovered, Girt was sure. Why hadn't he said something? What had he in mind to do about it?

It was coming home to Girt that he didn't know Bonney at all. Not this fellow — not the man called Billy the Kid. He had known — or thought he had known — Bill Bonney like a brother. But this fellow — this *new* Bonney — was a stranger; an unknown quantity entirely. Could the bounty dead Bill Brady had put upon young Bonney so have changed him?

Girt shook his head with a growl. His mind was full of questions — all of them without answers. But one thing was very certain; he had got to watch his step!

He had got to play this like it was poker, with the cards held close to his chest. Either that or go out feet first on a shutter. A deep game this, and one where his life could easy be forfeit. The blinders had come off now; he was beginning to sense the values. He was a lamb among a wolf-pack. He must bluff, and the bluff must be made to stick.

A lamb . . . ?

Girt scowled. A *weasel*, the girl had called him. All right! A weasel he'd be, by grab — and a weasel had teeth! He'd show her! And he'd show Bonney, too — he'd show the whole blame lot of them! The Romans had a name for it: cavvy-something emptor! Let the whole blame bunch beware!

Bonney wasted little time with Merrilyn in the hours that preceded darkness. Girt had expected him to spend the rest of the day with her just to show him who was brass-collar dog around these diggings. But instead the Kid went and squatted by the fire; aloof, absorbed in his own dark and secret reflections, he sat hunkered on his boot-heels and smoked one hand-rolled after another.

His face was a lean, dark blur as he sat huddled there by the hour, and Girt, covertly glancing at him from time to time, thought to find in him more wolf than the mad dog Bill Brady had named him. Even his posture resembled the wolf; and his grins and his sly, cunning scheming.

Dark tales came to mind as Girt eyed him; yarns that before he'd discounted. Things that he'd heard, stray whispers and hints. Ugly rumors. The country was rife with them — how he'd shot this man in the back — how he'd bamboozled that one's widow. The Kid, he knew, was reputed to have a girl in every placita; but in the past he had thought this just talk. It was said no girl was safe from him.

In the old days you could have counted the men who talked against the Kid on the fingers of one hand; now it was hard to find any who didn't. Even Chisum had turned against him. Only with the Mex pelados was Bonney held *buen amigos* — and even these eyed him nervously. The Kid had gone hog-wild, they said, and Girt was beginning to believe it.

Sometimes the Kid would bend a little forward to heave another stick on the fire. Such times Girt would see the heavy gun swing away from his leg, see its hostered bulk clear and sharp against the light. Would see the blaze-glow gleam along its handle. There were notches carved on that hickory stock, and knowledge of their meaning struck a chill through Girt.

But he did not forget his resolve. His schooled face showed blandly indifferent. He played seven-up with Bonney's gang; laughed loud and often as they did. But all the while his mind kept busy, shifting, discarding, speculating. If he were to get the best of Billy the Kid, he must be on his guard every minute. No more sulking. No more missteps — his next might be his last one.

He felt pretty sure now Bonney had been glad of an excuse to kill Valmora. He could not bring himself yet to believe the Kid had killed the breed deliberate — had cold-bloodedly planned the man's death. But he was not overlooking that possibility; and if desire for Merrilyn Matheson had moved the Kid to deal death once, there was a pretty grim possibility that same desire might move Bill Bonney again.

Girt kept his eyes skinned for trouble.

The card game seemed interminable. The afternoon wore out and dusk settled, blacker and blacker; and suddenly night was upon them. Bonney stretched and got up from the burnt-out fire; the men quit their game with a sigh. Bowdre chucked more wood on the coals and threw together a supper and they all pitched in without much talk and Girt drank his coffee down scalding.

In the fire-glow they rolled their smokes. "Time little girls went to bed," Bonney said, and looked over at Girt faintly mocking. Girt's cheeks felt hot, but he managed a laugh. "Yeah — run along, Merrilyn," he said with his eyes showing an alert vacuity.

Bonney, with a careless laugh, began pawing through his pockets. But when Merrilyn brushed the crumbs from her lap and got scornfully to her feet, he jumped off his rock with a grand low bow and she chucked him a mocking curtsey. "Sweet dreams," he said with a tight-lipped grin; and gave her no further attention.

His hands started through his pockets again while he looked Girt over coolly. The glance grew abruptly personal, intent and darkly probing. "Doggoned," he said, "if I ain't run plumb out of smokin', boy — got the makin's handy, hev you?"

Girt eyed him slanchways, wary, watchful. "Why, sure," he said, and got out his Durham. Scurlock was on his feet to the left, hands folded across his shirtfront. At the extreme right end of Girt's narrowed vision, Jim French was in the act of rising; and Hendry Brown, beside him, was leaning forward oddly.

Girt's Greener was on his horse and this looked mighty like a frame-up. Like a cat with a mouse, Bonney's eyes were; and his lean right hand was draped by a thumb to his belt buckle. Girt thought of Yorba Joe Valmora, and his blood knew a sudden cooling. His lips chucked back Bonney's grin, tight and wicked, and his drawl was a ringer for Bonney's. " 'D I ever tell you 'bout the time I dropped the Candlos boys, Bill? The way you-all are standin' kind of popped it into my mind. Ed Candlos was about like French there is, an' Wake —"

"We ain't got no time for windies," Scurlock cut in gruffly. "The Kid asked fer your tobacco, boy!" The rest were cat-still, watching.

Girt's nod was brief. "Here it is," he said, and tossed it.

Posed the way he'd been, Bonney's catching of the sack was an accomplishment of dexterity. His wiry body, turning slightly, never moved from its tracks, but his long left arm with a languid grace picked the packet right out of the air.

Whimsy edged his smile and his brows shot upward, mocking.

"What's the matter, boy? You sure are actin' proddy — fella'd think I was tryin' to hug you or somethin'. I ain't no dog to throw a bone at! Where the hell's your manners? What you got your hand on that gun for?"

"My manners suit me fine," Girt said, "an' my hand's right where I want it."

They stared across six feet of quiet; the Kid stock-still, blue eyes slit-slim in the fire-glow; Girt suspicious, wary.

Abruptly the Kid laughed, raspingly. "Dogged if I can get you, fella. Is that a chunk on your shoulder?" Girt didn't answer. He stood planted stiffly, uneasily conscious of the hard eyes boring into him; conscious of other things, none of them pleasant.

With the Durham sack strings in his teeth, the Kid peeled him off a paper, cupped it and with his free hand lined it with flakes of tobacco. Then he snicked the drawstrings shut; eyes a-glint, sent the sack snapping back to its owner.

Girt let it hit him — let it fall; kept his stare grim-fixed on Bonney.

Bonney said: "Say! You huntin' trouble?"

To say Girt wasn't scared would be lying. Suspense was like a knife blade slipping up his spine. Danger hair-triggered his muscles. His breath grew ragged and for one mad moment the clutch of his emotions threatened to drive him into a draw. For that wild interminable second he was like a man staring over a precipice — like a man holding on by a straw.

Then the tempestuous surge of the roaring blood passed; things fell back to their true perspective. To draw now surely spelled death, and he knew it. That was what Bill Bonney was angling for — he *wanted* Girt to draw!

Senses honed sharp, Girt schooled his tight face to a smiling; to a grimace that matched the Kid's own. He shrugged but kept the hand wrapped round his gun butt. And his drawl was enough like the Kid's that it might have been Bill Bonney speaking. "Aren't you loadin' me, Bill?" he asked. "You know I don't never hunt nothin'."

"Well, look at the bustard shake!" cried Brown; and Scurlock said with his Lucifer's sneer: "What's the matter, boy? Scared of your shadow?" Jim French loosed a hearty guffaw and even John Middleton grinned.

Girt said, "That ain't fright that makes my knees knock. That's brelderium I done picked up from prickly pear bites what I got that time I downed Thompson —"

"Kid ort to hire your tongue to keep the windmill goin'," Dave Ruddabaugh allowed; but Girt ignored him.

"Yes, I got that downin' Jim Thompson —"

"What was the matter with him — asleep?" sneered Scurlock. And Jim French said, "It sure must of been a slipp'ry day!"

But Girt didn't mind their insults — just so they didn't go gunning. Because once let the lead start to flying and Saint Pete's secretary might as well drag out the book and get the blotter ready.

Scurlock growled and slouched back down on his rock again; Jim French put a couple of fingers in his mouth and made a noise. Only dour Hendry Brown held his place without visible movement. There was a thoughtful light in his eyes that matched the Kid's.

Bonney stepped away from the fire. "Bowdre, fetch the bottle, will you? We'll all have a drink an' then I guess we better be ridin'," and he looked at Sasabe oddly.

Charlie brought up a demijohn. Hoisting it on his elbow, the Kid grunted: "Here's grit for the banty rooster, boys!" and lowered the contents a good two inches before coming up for air. Then he passed the jug to Scurlock. Hawkface spat and passed it on to Middleton; and so it went the rounds until it came to Girt.

The sheriff of Broken Stirrup had been scanning all the chances and finding none of them good. It looked to him like Bonney, having failed to lure him into a draw against the stacked guns of the owl-hooters, was determined to settle his hash some other way. And what way was better — or what way safer — than plugging a man while he was taking a swig from a bottle? Especially a bottle built like this one, which you had to throw your neck out of joint to get at it!

He laughed, affecting to find the idea funny. "Shucks, Bill," he said, "you know I never drink at night — too hard on my indigestion," and hoped they might believe it.

Bonney, it looked like, was willing. "Just as well," he grunted; but his blue eyes were bright and wicked. "I'm takin' the boys into Lincoln tonight — we're gettin' after that chore. But somebody's got to watch Twinkle-Eyes — she might take a itch to wander; might go off some place and get hurt. So" — the Kid's teeth gleamed in a tigerish smirk — "I'm namin' you to ride herd on her, Tinbadge; holdin' you responsible for her safety. And John," he said, widening his smirk to include Middleton, "you stay and lend Girt here a hand."

13

A prisoner — that's what he was! Might's well have put him in chains and been done with it! But no — Bonney's cat-and-mouse humor demanded that he wriggle; and he would, all right — helper John would see to that!

Girt cursed with a bitter fury.

To be cooped up in this pocket with Merrilyn and at the same time unable to help her had been a bitter pill for Girt, with his sheriff's star, to swallow. But it was twenty times worse, now the gang had gone off. He would never be able to make either the girl or her father understand why he didn't ride off with her pronto.

But there was reason, all right — damned sound reason, too! Free as the air, Bonney'd left him; he was not tied, he had his gun and cartridges. What a sly, vindictive buck Bill was! He could hardly have made Girt more uncomfortable, or made his position more embarrassing. There was nothing, apparently — nothing whatever, to keep Girt from saddling a couple of broncs and riding Merrilyn out of this.

But Girt was not deceived. There was Texas John Middleton.

One man, the girl would tell herself. No odds at all, she'd think, and find but one conclusion to Girt's damning lack of activity. What a hero he would look to be!

But Girt knew Middleton, and he could not forget the Kid's grin when naming Middleton to help him. Helper John was a dark-faced Texican, built like a slat, and with a pair of dexterous hands that never hung more than a half inch removed from the scabbarded Colts that flapped at his thighs. Middleton didn't tie his pistols down — he didn't *need* to; he could give most rannihans Jack and the game and beat them to the squeeze.

Tall and slouching, with shaggy black hair, the only neat thing about Texas John was the knife-gash mustache that rode his long upper lip and called second looks from the ladies. Oh, he was a handsome buck in a bold and cynical fashion. His chin-strapped hat and dangling cigarette gave him a tough-hombre look which his rep in no way denied.

And Girt knew that rep, for John was no shrinking violet and in certain circles was a much sought-after man. A horse thief and bank robber, he had departed Texas by the skin of his teeth; and the rangers were still on the watch for him. Nor had the just-finished war impaired his rep in any manner; he had filed four sleek new notches and had put at least that many more gents in bed — who were mighty damned glad to be there!

It was plain the Kid had not left the fellow behind for any ornament.

If Girt could only best the guy! If it had been anyone else — but Texas John was a hard-case hombre and wouldn't stand for no monkeyshines. When Middleton played, he played for keeps, and the thought was no spur to action.

There were a lot of slick ways, Girt reflected, for getting a guy out of tights. Only none of them was much good for cracking *his* nut. His problem seemed to be unique. Rescue was out of the question — there was nobody interested in rescuing him. He had matches in his pocket, but with Middleton's eager eye forever on him there was not much chance of kindling a fire — not much chance of doing anything else, either. Life with Middleton was hard lines and no mistake.

He had his gun and cartridges; but a

pistol around Texas John was about as useless as prodding the South Pole with a toothpick! John was not a guy you stood much chance in ever getting the drop on; nor could Girt consider with any enthusiasm the prospect of facing the guy in a duel. And he couldn't shoot Brother Middleton in the back.

So guns, it looked like, were out.

So were knives and other miscellaneous weapons.

Some way the freckled face of Darinthy-May got tangled in Girt's figuring. A good girl, Darinthy — except she was too ganglin'-like and bony, and you could use her hair to read by, and it would keep you up all night to count the freckles on her face. But a good girl right enough — plumb honest. And a hard worker, too — she had to be, Girt thought, to keep up her hard-drinking father.

He wondered what Darinthy would do if faced with this situation. But the answer evoked by Darinthy's forthright personality was no kind of help to Girt. Might's well ask what Bonney would have done. You couldn't play that tune on Middleton!

Girt couldn't anyhow. Strategy was the word, all right; he'd have to throw John off his guard.

He said: "Guess I'll hit the hay," real casual. But Middleton only grinned. "Yeah?" he said. "Well, guess again — y'u fo'gettin' Bonney's o'dehs?"

So Girt slacked off into silence, sulkily glared at the fire. That was the trouble with these Texas squirts — they'd learned all the tricks in the cradle.

If he could just get shut of the cuss for a second — But there wasn't a chance. John wasn't letting him out of his eyesight, not even for personal problems.

"Hell!" Girt said at last. "I got to have a drink."

"Sure," John told him, getting up. "I could use a drink myself. Lead the way — the spring's over there to your left."

Girt struck off, his thoughts flying round like a couple dry beans in a bottle. If John would only —

But when they reached the spring Middleton said, "You first, boy — I wasn't borned yesterday."

So Girt with an oath hunkered down on his belly and took a few swigs for appearance. He was dipping his neck for another when he jumped with a cry and rolled sideway. "Look out, Tex! — *sidewinder!*" And he rocked to and fro in a dither with both hands clapped to his thigh.

But Texas John didn't get nervous. "Tough!" His grin was broad and knowing. "An' not a sawbones in forty mile!"

Girt played it a little longer, then got sheepishly to his feet. "Aw, hell," he growled, "you're too slick for me," and Middleton nodded, chuckling.

"I been around, boy."

"I guess you've heard the owl hoot?"

"A time or two," John said modestly. "Now let's cut out this monkey stuff —"

"What about that girl?" Girt asked. The Kid had built her a little brush hut off to one side of the pocket. It was to this she had gone after supper. "Don't you reckon mebbe we better take a squint —"

"I reckon," Middleton said, "y'u better be savin' that breath to cool yo' beans with. That skirt ain't goin' no place. Drop anchor, boy; git over there by that fire an' quit yo' damn junin' around!"

With a sigh Girt did as bidden. He eyed his new star glumly. For a lawman he was about as helpless as a new-sheared sheep in a snowdrift! It sure did burn his gizzard to be ordered around like a mozo; but there was a glint in the Texican's eye that said he was all fed up with fooling.

He sat down across the fire from Girt and from time to time replenished the blaze with lengths of mesquite or grease-wood. Girt got to staring at the tunnel mouth and abruptly an idea struck him. He turned it over in his mind and, the more he studied it, the more convinced he became that it was the one chance to get the girl out of here.

He watched the Texican throw wood on the fire; let his glance play idly around. He found what he was looking for finally — a fair-sized rock he could heave good; and next time Middleton reached for a stick he let the rock drive at the tunnel mouth.

It was slick, well timed; he was still, slumped over dolefully, when the outlaw's eyes raked a glance at him. The rock struck with a clatter abruptly drowned in a girl's shrill scream.

They whirled together, he and Middleton; Girt's jaw was slack with amazement. Merrilyn's voice! What the hell was she doing in the tunnel? How'd she gotten there?

He met Middleton's stare maliciously. "Told you," he said loudly, "that we ought to of took a look!"

But Middleton wasn't listening. He was off with a curse for the tunnel. Girt piled after him. But not three jumps had he taken when the Texican whirled, eyes slitted, and his gun jabbed hard in Girt's stomach.

"Haul up! I'll take care of this! Git back to that fire 'fore y'u wish y'u had!"

So perforce Girt, muttering, went back.

It was hard, bitter hard, to see a good plan wrecked so completely. That stone had not helped Merrilyn a great deal either. Looked like she'd been about to cut loose on her own hook; his rock must have plain scared hell out of her. But cry-*minie!* If she'd stayed in the brush like she should have, he'd of had them both out of here by this time!

Far as that went, if he didn't have her to get lathered about, he could get himself free in a jiffy. It was her — the fact she was a girl, that got things tangled so. If it wasn't for her he wouldn't be *trying* to get out of here; he'd still be *buen amigos* with Bonney. Fact is, if it wasn't for her he wouldn't be sheriff — he'd have turned the job down in the first place.

And so Girt spluttered; and was still spluttering when Middleton came tramping into the firelight, shoving the disheveled girl before him. She was still defiant — not a doubt of it; only Texas John's tight grip on her arm was securing her rebellious obedience. He was all fed up with fooling, as the scowl on his face gave evidence; and he marched her straight back to the wickiup, strode grimly inside of it with her.

When he stepped out some seconds later and came surging up to the fire he was breathing heavy and there was a glint in his eye that promised mischief if anything else went haywire. "I've tied her up," he said, "an' she's goin' to stay tied," and he looked at Girt plumb hostile. "An' if I thought fer one holy minute —"

"Aw, cry-*minie!*" Girt growled, disgusted. "Go roll your hoop awhile, will you?"

"You're goin' to have yo' hoop rolled, boy, 'f I have any more monkeyshines out of you!"

Conversation languished then. But suddenly Texas John was up again, up barelipped and snarling. Once more sound had come from the tunnel; new sound, *hoof* sound — definite. A gun threw its wicked glint from each of Middleton's fists. Soft as silk he purred: "No matter who this is, y'u keep yo' yap shut, boy, an' leave me do the talkin'. One peep out o' y'u about yon skirt an' that peep'll be yo' last!"

14

Girt, at this moment ready to see in any interruption — in the intrusion of any third party or element — an advantage to himself, was leaning forward excitedly, keening with ill-concealed eagerness the deep-banked shadows piled in curdled chaos about the tunnel's mouth. But the man who seconds later came jogging a black horse out of it was the very last fellow on earth he'd have chosen just then to see — Cash Benson!

He would sooner have seen the devil himself than this cause of all his troubles. For it was Benson's orders that had moved Valmora — Benson's desires that animated half the crooks in the Territory; whose word governed Broken Stirrup's sporting gentry, whose guile supplied the Mescaleros fire-water, whose agile brain and implacable nature made him overlord of all the rustlers — Benson! *the man Girt had warned from the country!*

Nor had Benson forgotten that warning!

To say the man was surprised would be the underest of understatements. He pulled up his horse and stared; and suddenly a wide grin bared his teeth maliciously.

"Well! Well Well!" he said, and chuckled. "Been hopin' I'd run across you. We parted kind of abruptly if memory serves me right, and — but this is *fine!*"

He roved a glance across Middleton then; said, "Hello, John," rather indifferently, and looked Girt over again with pleasure — with the hungry sort of pleasure a shaggy wolf might accord a rabbit.

Girt's grin was without enthusiasm.

If things had been dark with him before, they were black now as a dead steer's gullet.

It sure looked like his goose was cooked.

"Cry-*minie!*" he told himself; and resolved if he ever got a hand to trigger he would do his shooting right away and talk things over after.

But resolving was one thing. Performance was another; and performing heroic feats with a sixgun after all your life being — well, anyways, just a mite shy about such things, was apt to be something in the nature of sprinkling salt on a meadow lark's tail!

And, unfortunately, that was Girt's trouble. That he had gotten away with his pose of leather-slapper during what part he had played in the just-finished Murphy-Chisum feud was owing entirely to the fact he'd only been one of many; his many maneuvers with pistols had been sheerest, boldest bluff! But bluffing now held no jubilee prospect — let him once clap hand to iron *now* and he'd damned well better use it!

It was the *Greener* he'd used on Crispin — that had so boosted Girt's stock with Clay Matheson. If only he had that shotgun now he would give these birds something to tell about — But the Greener was on his saddle, and the saddle was a hump on the kak-pole at the farthest side of the pocket.

He could almost taste Boot Hill, Girt thought; and Boot Hill was in Cash Benson's mind, if a man were to judge by his look.

The rustler boss swung down from his horse, trailed the reins and was making toward Girt when a cry stopped him short in his tracks — a girl's cry! — *Merrilyn's!*

"Help! *Help!*"

The repeated word rang crystal clear, desperate in its urgency.

Hopes hammering, Girt flicked a look at Middleton. The outlaw's face was grayly set, was hard — gone stiff as bee's wax. There was a gaunt erectness in his stance that told of wire-taut nerves; and that look stared from his eyes that watched Benson's every blink with a dire and strained intensity. And Middleton's hands were clawed, were spraddled above his thighs like buzzards ready to make a dive.

It was plain that Benson observed the pose; he gave it a careless smile. "A lady, eh? Some new flame of the Kid's, I imagine," he said blandly. Then: "Come, come! Brush your feathers down, John — I'm not looking for secondhand fillies. There's not but one skirt in the Territory I'd give a snap of the fingers for; and," he said, smile widening, "I've got her safe where I want her."

John, grinning sheepish, came out of his crouch; threw a couple more sticks on the fire. And he was that way, just straightening up, when Benson pronounced: "But just in case . . . we'll take a look at this dame anyway."

Caught off guard, Middleton hung there, slack-jawed, stiff and staring — unwieldy as the tangled mind so neatly trapped by Benson's faster thinking.

It was Benson's hand that draped a gun stock now; Texas John was proved a fool.

There was a lesson here, and Girt observed it. Observed Cash Benson's grin; the throaty chuckle that broke from him at the Texican's black, balked rage.

Benson tired of his sport abruptly. "Move along, John; lead the way. We'll take a look at Bonney's beauty. . . . Ah? Beg pardon?"

Middleton was like a bulldog. He planted himself there lumpishly, legs spraddled, jaw set. Dogged. He'd not go a step. He said so.

No laugh curled Benson's lips back now. "I think you win," he said quietly; and Texas John, with a bitter, choked oath, lurched off toward the girl's brush wickiup.

But Benson's soft call checked him. "Just a second, friend John. You'll have no need of those guns for a while — hump over there, Sheriff, an' lift 'em."

Girt did so without any jawing. This Benson was no kind of jasper to tinker with. Girt might be green, but he was quick to learn, and two examples were plenty; he had not forgotten Benson's trick on him, and Middleton's plight was enlightening. He lifted the Texican's pistols; gingerly gripping them, alertly waited further orders.

"Chuck 'em into the brush."

Ignoring Middleton's cursing, Girt heaved them as far as he could.

"Now throw your own after them," Benson ordered; and with a sigh Girt did as bidden.

"That's fine; you learn pretty fast, boy. Okay, John," Benson purred amiably. "We'll visit Bonney's girl now."

15

"Got her hogtied, eh?" Benson murmured. "Pity you didn't gag her — bit short-sighted, wasn't it?" He grinned at Middleton's discomfiture. "No need of you introducing us; I've an idea we're acquainted — though I've not had an opportunity of seeing the lady in pants before. Miss Matheson, ain't it? What a jolly reunion, Merrilyn!"

Under the rustler's amused scrunity, Merrilyn shrank as much as her bonds would allow her. There was a fright in her eyes that gritted Girt's teeth; and her cheeks were chalk-white, twisted.

Benson chuckled. "I've a wish your father might see you; it might bring him to heel a bit quicker," he said. "After all, what is money where you're concerned? I believe I'll have you send word to him — John, here, will be glad to carry it; a description of life in the Kid's camp —"

The girl's low gasp was lost in Middleton's growled: "What the hell y'u talkin' about?"

"Why, forfeiture, John," Benson drawled urbanely. "Ransom. Did you suppose I had gone to all this trouble just to fill in a little spare time? That was not my reason, I assure you — nor was it to provide more sport for Bonney. The young lady's father — case you haven't been told — is a banker, John; the biggest banker in the Territory. Ought to pay rather well, don't you think, to get such a baggage back safely?"

Middleton stared with fallen jaw. It was plain he'd not guessed Merrilyn's standing.

But Girt had no thought or energy to waste on Texas John at the moment. Of prime consideration in his mind was the problem of getting Merrilyn out of this — and that was like to take all the king's horses, he thought bitterly.

Benson had all the edges. More, he had the advantage of a gun. But there, Girt thought, might lie the answer to this problem; that gun might be the thing with which Girt could turn defeat into victory. Knowing Middleton and himself disarmed, Benson might just possibly get careless. It was a chance worth watching for, anyway.

But Benson was not overlooking anything.

"Just mind where you put your hands,

young fellow," he drawled sardonically at Girt. "I could tie you, of course, if I wanted to bother. But shootin's a heap easier and has the advantage of being permanent."

He lifted the gun from his hip and twirled it around by its trigger guard while he looked at Middleton as though seriously debating that hombre's fate. Then: "John," he said softly, "get the ropes off that girl." Just like that; no threats, no warnings. But the alacrity with which the scowling Middleton obeyed — the care and circumspection he put into that obedience — told Girt plainly at what height stood Cash Benson in the Texican's estimation.

And then Merrilyn Matheson, still togged in Bonney's charro duds, stood swaying, free of her ropes — stood white of face as a bed-sheet, like she'd fall at the puff of a breath.

And Girt sprang forward, thinking to catch her — might have, had not Cash Benson's pistol suddenly dug him in the stomach. Benson said: "Just keep your shirt on, sonny; she ain't needin' no help you can give. Get back against that wall!"

And Girt fell back with a bitter scowl, muttering to himself. There was nothing else he *could* do — Benson had the gun.

171

But it was downright humiliating to be treated like some Mexican's yellow hound! Bottled rage threatened to choke him. The look in his eye would have split a post; but Benson only smiled.

Girt remembered something then. That was no way to handle Benson. Strategy was what he needed; he must play this smooth and tricky. He must keep his temper — take a page from Bonney. "Rage only gets guys planted," Bonney had said the other day; and the Kid was right.

But it was hard — bitter hard, for a man of Sasabe's forthright nature to resort to flimflam trickery. He was impulsive, frank and open, unused to twists and dodges, to dissembling and the like. But he could learn! By grab, he *would* learn! He would play it foxy. Like the weasel this girl had called him. *Jackrabbit!* — she'd called him that one, also. He smarted with remembrance of it. But just you wait! *He'd* show 'em!

Benson, with a look of cold amusement, drawled: "Watch out there, Tinbadge. If you don't tone that scowl down you'll bust your nutcrackers sure. What's the matter? Bellyache?"

"Guess I *did* look kind of daunsy," Girt admitted, smiling sheepish. "Trouble with

me is I'm too dang tender-hearted —
always worryin' about the other guy —
b'out the grief he's pilin' up. But you
ought to know what you're doin'," he said,
thin lips streaking a smile. "You're over
twenty-one. I guess you're dry behind the
ears."

Benson frowned. The slanchways glance
he put on Girt was intently probing — calculating. There was a wonder back of that
stare that proved the rustler uneasy; Girt
had gotten beneath his guard.

"Well, let him wonder!" Girt thought
grimly. "If he wonders enough —"

But Benson appeared through with wondering. The cold amusement rode his high
cheekbones again; showed him briskly
ready for business. "I —" he began, then
stared at Middleton as though considering
some new notion that had come to him.
Then his thoughtful glance sharpened.
"Take her out to the fire, John," he murmured, and didn't have to tell the man
twice.

As the girl and Middleton moved past
him, Benson said to Girt: "You, too! And
save some of that sorrow for yourself, my
friend; you're going to need it before I've
done with you."

But Girt grinned back at him brashly;

loosed a chuckle as he stepped through the door. And a hint of the Kid's saddle-bound swagger crept into his walk as he strode carelessly up to the fire.

Merrilyn's eyes went to him wonderingly; and, catching Benson's narrowed glance upon him, Girt saucily flicked her a wink. He had 'em going at last, by grab! He'd give them something to think about!

Benson said to the girl: "Go fetch in your saddle — and don't lay yourself open to snake-bite hunting for any exit. There's only one way out of here; the tunnel you came in by. I'll be keeping my eye on that."

Girt said: "Sure, go ahead. Better humor him."

"That's enough out of you!" snapped Benson. "Hurry up, girl — get a wiggle on!" And he leveled his pistol for business, dropping his road-agent monkeyshines.

Girt knew a sudden elation. Rustler Benson was getting nervous! The sheriff's paraded nonchalance was having its effect, was undermining Cash Benson's confidence. He was bound to suspect Girt possessed of some adverse knowledge, and that suspicion was engendering in the man a premonition of disaster. He was in a sudden sweat to get out of Bonney's rendezvous; and Girt grinned at him joyously.

"No need to rush," Girt chuckled. "You got the whole night to work in; the Kid's took his gang off to Lincoln —"

"Shut your yap!" Benson's look was ugly. "Texas," he said to Middleton as the girl came back dragging her saddle, "grab that rope an' get her a horse — an' be goddam spry about it!"

"Tck! Tck! Tck!" Girt clucked. "Such haste! Ain't you never heard haste makes —"

Wham!

Benson's gun spurted flame and the sound of its slug was a whistle beside Girt's ear. But though goosebumps broke out all over him, Girt gave the man a broad grin; and Benson cursed, convinced that noise was what Girt had been fishing for.

"One more crack out of you," Benson breathed, "an' I'll beat you into a splatter. Hurry up!" he growled at Middleton. "Any damn horse'll do!"

He reached down, jerked the rifle from Merrilyn's saddle; glance glued to Girt's face every second. "Better stick to your sixgun," Girt chuckled.

But under his forced levity he was racking his brain in a fury. Once let Benson get the girl on a bronc and out of here and he'd have all his work to do over!

Someway he must try to stop them —
must!

Middleton came tugging a horse into the
glow of the dying embers. Benson, lip
caught between the gleam of teeth, raked
his scowl about him wickedly. "Toss the
girl your rope an' throw some more wood
on that fire!"

He seemed to think Middleton the more
dependable man for carrying out his
orders; probably because John was the
more mature man and therefore liable to
exercise caution, whereas Girt he probably
considered a brash young fool, reckless
enough to try anything. The notion made
Girt chuckle.

Benson's face went darker. "Go on,
laugh while you've got a chance —"

"Look out," Girt grinned, "that scowl
will be bustin' your nut-crackers! What's
the matter? Got a bellyache? I thought you
was a badman, Benson! But shucks, you're
just plain bogeyman — the kind women
use to scare kids with!" And he went off
into a roar of laughter. "Cash Benson —
bogeyman!" he guffawed.

"Bogeyman, eh? We'll see!"

The rustler's tone was a promise; and
Girt, suddenly quaking inside him, had a
hunch it was no vain boast.

16

Grimly Girt scanned the chances. There weren't any chances to speak of. Texas John and himself were unarmed; Benson had a gun and would not be squeamish about using it — to judge by his look, he'd enjoy an excuse.

But would he? Might not Benson, too, be bluffing?

Well, he might; but Girt didn't think so. Girt's actions may have suggested to Benson he'd welcome a little noise; but if Benson found the going too rough, he would shoot his way out of here anyway. So far as he knew, Girt and the Kid were amigos. Girt's impulse to consolidate his position from that front abruptly faded as he recalled how the rustler had found Merrilyn. The girl had been tied — that wouldn't augur much friendliness between the Broken Stirrup sheriff and Bonney.

Girt hunted some other avenue down which he might crowd his luck.

He knew his paraded nonchalance had

rattled Benson sort of; but any advantage accruing from that would be offset by the rustler boss's risen vigilance. Benson was watching him like a hawk — was ready and maliciously waiting any move Girt might make.

But Texas John Middleton's extreme care in obeying each of Benson's orders to the letter had given Girt something to think about. This care was an education — it was a clear insight into owlhoot psychology. Middleton, as tough a buck as had ever rifled a bank teller's till, was a sure-fire, double-acting engine as long as he had the edge. But after Benson had grabbed that edge away from him, all his toughness had vanished. John Middleton right at this moment was meeker than Old Man Moses!

So how, Girt wondered, would Benson react if ever the drop got away from him? Might not the rustler boss, too, fold up like a leaf if his advantage were cut from under him?

It was something to think about, anyway.

Only, trouble was, the means for getting Benson's advantage away looked to be scarce as hens' teeth in Arizona!

Benson seemed to guess Girt's thoughts; the suave grin spread his lips again. "Got it figured out yet, Tinbadge?"

"Sure!" Girt declared. "You watch my smoke!"

But Benson's glance turned jeering. "I've heard mills screak before," he said. "You'll need more than wind to cut this one. Get over there now with your back to the fire — that's right! Now spread your arms out sideways!"

Girt felt like a dadblamed scarecrow. And the hell of it was, this fencepost pose gave Benson an added advantage; with the fire at his back, if Girt wriggled a toe Cash Benson would know the fact pronto.

Another thing — Girt couldn't stand this way forever. If he held the pose another ten minutes, cramp would ruin his gun hand. Already his nerves were jumping. His stretched arms felt heavy as lead.

One other thought came to torment him: the Kid and his still-absent owlhooters. There'd be no aid for Girt in the return of smiling Bill Bonney!

The fire's heat was scorching, but a cold sweat beaded Girt's forehead. This sure was one damned hell of a fix in which for a tinbadge to find himself!

And there wasn't no way out of it. Every trick went to Cash Benson; every trick but — Wait!

Girt's lean jaw snapped forward. There might be one slim chance left yet! Girt remembered the rustler's curse; his expression after firing the shot that had whistled past Girt's cheek. If Girt had guessed wrong — if Benson, not knowing where the Kid and his gang were — worried lest their sudden return bring havoc to his plans, dared not for fear of attracting them fire save in dire emergency. . . .

Girt eyed Benson and spat.

"A hell of an owlhooter *you* are!" he jeered, and hauled in his arms and stood flexing them, boldy and brashly — dead reckless. He presented a picture of defiant contempt; but inside he was shivering, quaking, bracing himself for the smash of hot lead that might rip from the rustler boss's pistol.

But not a shot came. Benson's smile was indulgent. "I never professed to be one."

"No," Girt sneered, "you bet you didn't! You ain't got the guts to be a badman! Oh, sure," he said with a scorn even Merrilyn might not have been ashamed of, "you can scare these two-bit squirts like Texas John, here, easy — but a kid with a pop-gun could do that much! Put you up again' the gen-u-wine article, Benny, an' you'd sure fold up like a tent!"

Benson's cheeks took a heightened color that did not result from any sunset. Texas John looked like he couldn't decide if he'd ought to laugh or walk over and bust Girt's face in.

But Benson's mind worked faster — may even have grasped Girt's purpose. He displayed his teeth in what was doubtless intended for a smile.

But Girt had hardly got started. Observing Cash's gargoyle grimace, he declared: "That look brings to mind the way the Chessycat grinned when the gol'fish stuck in its throat. Hell's fire, Benny! whyn't you trade that wishbone off for a backbone? When a real man takes you up on your brags —"

"I guess," Benson said real thick-like, "you're thinkin' of that damn Kid. Well, let me tell —"

"Who — Bonney? *That wart?* Not on your tin-type, bucko! I'm talkin' about — me! I reckon you felt slicker'n a frog's belly when you had that half-breed slasher, Valmora, wrap that pick handle round my cabeza. But let me tell you, if you hadn't left in such a lather, I'd of shown you how to *use* that pick handle, mister! Why, you ain't got the nerve of a jackrabbit! Go on, you pouter pigeon — *scowl;* I'm goin' to show you up right now, by grab! I'm goin' to rope me out a horse an' then I'm takin' Miz' Merrilyn out of here!"

And without another word Girt wheeled; went tramping across the pocket.

It would have been hard to tell who was the most amazed — John Middleton or Merrilyn Matheson. Cash Benson never fired a shot but stood there glaring, furious. What the Texican and Merrilyn could not understand was exactly the thing Girt had banked on. He had sold Benson the impression he wanted noise; and Cash wouldn't fire if hell froze — he didn't dare! Girt, by his bluff, had convinced him that Bonney's whole gang was someplace just out of earshot — that, had he fired, he'd have brought them running. Cash could not afford that. He must have figured, too, that Girt would not pull out and leave the girl here; and he couldn't get out anyway unless he left by the tunnel. So what the hell?

Cash's fleering smile was back again. He eyed the girl maliciously. "Throw her hull on that bronc," he told John, "an' mind you yank them girths tight."

While Middleton, glance still fogged with bafflement got to work cinching up the girl's saddle, Benson stood with a thin half-smile and watched Girt striding corral-ward. It would not be long, his expression said, before the sheriff abandoned his tomfoolery. Indeed, the caliber of Benson's smile suggested he found it hard to believe Girt would even *go* to the corral when it was so plain his ruse had failed.

But Girt *did* go there. His gaunt form made a dim-seen bluer against the aspen rails; and suddenly the smile fell off the rustler's face. With a curse he yanked his sixgun — triggered frantically.

But Benson, confident that Girt, unarmed, had been bluffing, had held his fire too long. Too late he had seen his error. Not till the sheriff had reached the corral had Benson guessed Girt's real purpose.

He emptied the pistol vainly. Rage unsteadied his aim and the rekindled fire between them was no aid in spotting Girt's moving shape. Benson hurled the pistol down; with an oath snatched up the girl's rifle.

But too late again — the tables were turned. Like a toothless wolf he took to the brush with Texas John crowding his heels — spurred on by the crash of Girt's Greener!

17

For the fourteenth time in Girt's bashful presence, Merrilyn Matheson retold how the sheriff had saved her from the machinations of the Kid and Cash Benson; how, with a brash effrontery well-nigh incredible, he had bluffed Benson out of his aces and with what was comparable to a bob-tailed flush had joggled defeat into victory. How he'd driven those tough monkeys, Benson and Texas John, to cover, had flung her aboard the horse John Middleton had saddled, hopped aboard Benson's own bronc and, with Greener still banging, gotten her safely out of the pocket.

And for the fourteenth time Banker Clay Matheson said: "By God, boy, I'll be damned!"

Girt's grin showed a young fellow's deep embarrassment.

"Shucks," he mumbled, "no gent craves to buck a shotgun; Jim Dolan proved that in Lincoln, time he made the boys back down from the necktie party they were gettin' set to give Bill Bonney. What I done wasn't anything. I just used my head is all — I wasn't tryin' to be no nickel-plated hero."

Clay Matheson gave him a long slow look and shook his head. "What were you trying to do?"

"Why, just what I *did* do, I reckon," Girt told him, fidgeting uneasily. "Tryin' to live up to the confidence you put in me —"

"Well, you done it, boy!" Clay Matheson said, and swore. Then his glance swept up and there was considerable speculation in the look that probed young Sasabe's high, flushed cheeks. "Speakin' of Bonney though . . . I'm kind of interested in what Merry said about that plan of his for riflin' that store in Lincoln. McSween's, you said it was, didn't you?" he asked, flicking a look at the girl. "Don't seem like even the Kid could be bad enough to rob his employer's widow —"

"Oh," remarked Girt generously, "I expect that was jest another one of his whoppers — he gets a bang out of workin' folks up. Likes to see their eyes bug out; but he ain't so bad — not really. Kind-hearted as the day is long —"

"Sure," cut in Clay Matheson dryly. "It was certainly kind of him, lavishing so much of his time and attention on my daughter!"

"Oh, *that!*" Girt said. "He was jest hoorahin' me, I guess; he knew I was in a lather to get back. As for that store-raidin' business, I expect you'll find that was nothing but hot air. Mebbe Brown an' French knew I was handy an' made the whole thing up —"

"Mebbe," Matheson echoed. "Only, as it happens, McSween's store *was* looted — just the other night; I've got a letter here from Peppin. Said I'd better keep my eyes peeled. Seems to think the Kid's headed over this way."

Girt's swallower stuck under the banker's sudden sharp scrutiny.

When he got it working again he said, "It's funny *I* ain't had no word of it! Prob'ly just another wild rumor — country's full of 'em."

Girt said it blithely, but it did not brush his hackles down. If the Kid should ramp into Torrance County — but he wouldn't! Of course he wouldn't — *not after what had happened!*

Girt shifted his weight uneasily. He wished he could be sure of it. But a man, he was beginning to realize, couldn't be sure of anything where young Bill

Bonney was concerned.

"What I'm worried about," he scowled, "is that dang handbill Dudley's posted. Suppose —"

"I wouldn't fret none over that," Clay Matheson told him. "There's a motion up in Washington right now to have him broken. Wouldn't surprise me if the old fool got cashiered. He's got it coming if any man ever had! Between you and me, I don't believe the Governor's sitting any too easy."

He picked up the papers on his desk, adjusted his glasses. "Well," he said, eyeing his daughter fondly, "you kids run along now; the Old Man's busier'n hell today. . . . Uh — Sasabe! If you're not tied up this evening, how about taking dinner at our place? . . . Tut, tut! Glad to have you," and with a goodnatured grin he waved them out of the office.

Girt, in a dither of delight over the new, exalted station he appeared to hold in this girl's opinion, would have spent the rest of the day with Merrilyn, had she let him. But Merry — she had told him he could call her that — was going shopping and, "After all," she said, eyes twinkling, "you've got your work to do, you know. But tonight" —

187

she paused and laughed deliciously — "tonight — well, you come along and see!"

She made the prospect sound quite intimate, tumultuously disturbing; and Girt's cheeks flushed with pleasure. He squeezed her hand in his big one — felt her return the pressure. There was a lively color in her cheeks and her eyes shone bright as stars as she laughed up at him. "Tonight, then," she said huskily, and before he could stop her was gone.

He scowled; grinned after her ruefully. She sure made a man feel important! And that look he'd caught in her eyes just then — He laughed, intoxicated. Laughed with a sudden pride of her. There weren't many girls like her in this world!

He set off with his feet in the clouds.

Where he went, what he did or why, he never could remember; but a sudden rude bump jarred him back to earth. He scowled at the man before him.

A fellow so fat a man would have to throw a diamond hitch to keep him in the saddle. Lacing elephant hands across his robust girth, this citizen gave back Girt's glower with interest. "Whew — pick me up, Gerty!" he wheezed indignantly. "Whyn'tcha look where you're goin'?"

"If it comes to that, whyn't *you*?" Girt

snapped, and shoved past him without further jawing. Just because the fool was fat didn't give him a lease of the sidewalk!

But after a few steps Girt's resentment faded. He got to thinking about food somehow and realized he was hungry. He looked at his shadow and swore, surprised. Two hours past lunchtime already — no wonder his stomach was howling!

He was feeling at peace with himself and the world by the time he reached the Honky-Donk Hash House. The way folks stared and looked after him was ointment for almost anything. Seemed like he was getting to be quite a personage! He wasn't, of course — was the same old Girt; but he enjoyed knowing people noticed him. "That's him!" he heard one fellow say. "See the star? That's Sheriff Girt Sasabe! Yeah — real double-actin' engine. I'd like to seen Cash Benson's mug. . . ." And another man called, "H'are yuh, Girt?" and Girt waved him an airy greeting, though he didn't know the guy from Adam.

That was the way life went, he mused; that was what fame did for a man. A lucky break and you got your name in every guy's mouth — became *buen amigos* with the world.

With the world, perhaps, but not with Darinthy-May Tolliver, who was a nonconformist and didn't give a rap what the world thought about anything.

Girt saw her as soon as he stepped in the door; and was glad there weren't but two or three late eaters present. For the old mocking look was plain in her eye and her opening words were a warning.

"Howdy, Tinbadge," she said, and then, eyes springing wide: "Heavenly days! Ain't you bought a new hat yet?"

With a frown Girt dragged off his horse-thief hat, stared at it suspiciously. "What's the matter with this one?"

"Oh, nothing, I guess. Only I didn't suppose it'd still fit you."

Girt clapped the hat back on his head with a scowl and buried his face in a menu.

"What's the idea," pursued Darinthy-May relentlessly, "puttin' wear an' tear on that card? As if you didn't know what kind of chow we sling here!"

Girt scowled under the three late eaters' inspection, blushed furiously and gave his order in a mutter.

"Got your coffin ordered yet?"

She asked it brusquely as she set the grub before him; and laughed sarcastically as he turned inquiring eyes upon the steaming cup of java she had just placed by his plate. "You heard me right the first time — I said 'coffin'."

"Oh!" Girt managed a wilted grin. "You're thinkin' of Colonel Dudley — them handbills of his, I reckon —"

"That fathead! I wouldn't waste that much energy," she declared acidulously. "I'm talkin' about Cash Benson, if you ain't already grasped it. You don't think he's goin' to take this layin' down, I hope? He had a real investment in that jane, an' won't much cotton to losin' it. D'you know how much he was askin'? *Forty-five thousand dollars!*"

"Forty-five thousand *what?*" asked Girt, jaw dropping.

"Dollars, Tinbadge — coin of the realm." Darinthy-May appeared to be enjoying Girt's consternation. "That's a pile of money, all right, but Matheson could pay it; he's a banker, ain't he? Biggest in the land. I expect that's why you're playin' up to him. That's your own business, though, and if you don't care what folks are sayin', why, that's your business too, I reckon. But hell on cartwheels! I wouldn't be *no* man's monkey-on-a-stick!"

And, with that parting shot, she flounced

off into the kitchen, leaving Girt to the customers' laughter.

It was in no complacent frame of mind that, half an hour later, Girt stalked into the sheriff's office, a four-by-eight cubbyhole affixed to the county jail. He was in a sod-pawing mood and sight of the hombre parked on his desk did nothing to put his hackles down. It was the fat man he'd bumped into on the street.

"Whew — pick me up, Gerty! So *you're* the sheriff, are you? My stars! I thought you'd croaked or somethin' — I been waitin' here three hours —"

"Nobody asked you to!" Girt broke in rudely. "You didn't need to do no waitin' on *my* account."

"That's where you're wrong," the visitor panted, beaming. "If you're Sheriff Sasabe — Say! that was funny, me bumpin' into you back yonder an' never guessin' who it was . . . er —"

"Was it?"

The fat man mopped his triple chins. He looked at Girt reproachfully. "After all, I'm tryin' to do you a favor, mister. You don't need to take my head off." He laced his elephant hands across his paunch and heaved a sigh that set the reward posters

192

rattling, "Just goes to prove what I've allus said. . . ."

But Girt didn't rise to the bait. With a disgruntled grimace the big gent pulled a stick of gum from his flannel shirt pocket and, paper and all, absent-mindedly put it in his mouth.

That got hold of Girt's interest and he watched expectantly for the fellow to spit it out, but with a cow-like placidity the man chewed on till Girt at last growled:

"What's your handle an' what'd you want to see me about?"

The big face brightened. "Nettleton's the name — Yaggy Nettleton. You better take me on, pardner; they sure sound good together. Girt an' Yaggy — like ham an' eggs, eh?" and Nettleton guffawed loudly.

"Very funny," Girt said dryly. "If you've any business here, state it. If not, clear out — make yourself scarce."

With a deal of wheezing and grunting the big fellow hoisted himself from Girt's desk. He looked at Girt and sniffed, chewing his wrapped gum noisily. "So you're the new sheriff, eh, Johnny, my lad? Looks like they been robbin' the cradle." And he sniffed again. "I might of knowed from the talk you was too rattleheaded to even drive nails in a snowbank. Hell!" He stood, arms

193

planted akimbo, and looked Girt square in the eye. "You goin' to hire me or ain't you?"

"No!" Girt said without compromise. "When I'm wantin' an ornament I'll get one that takes less room."

"You'd no call to say that, young feller." The fat man's sigh was reproachful. "I'd hoped we could get on agreeable, seem's we're both goin' to use this office. Don't think," he said, holding a hand up, "you're the only star around this horizon — 'cause you ain't! Take a squint at this!" He slapped his hide vest back from his shirt; and Girt, looking, loosed a quick oath.

"Where'd you get that badge?"

"I got it, all tight; an' she's permanent." Nettleton's smile was sardonic. "I'm chief deputy here whether you like it or not; an' if you wasn't so smart I could do you some good. It happens I'm Axtell's nephew —"

"The Governor's nephew!" cried Girt, taken aback. "You're Governor Axtell's *nephew?*"

"Sure," Yaggy said; "but it ain't my fault." And his chuckle was so infectious Girt found himself chuckling with him. "Put 'er there!" Yaggy said, and extended his hand; and with an oath Girt shook it vigorously.

"You can fry me for a Chinaman!" Girt said; and the fat man said: "Me, too!"

Girt was in a lather when the butler took his hat — a brand new sixty-dollar one — that night at the Matheson residence; but the dinner went off like a log on greased skids even though Mrs. Matheson's eyebrows like to have jumped clean into her hair when Girt used his steak knife on the butter dish and then tried the same blade on his peas. But Girt never noticed in the excitement of being near Merrilyn; and when once or twice conversation appeared to lag, he spiced it up with some jokes the barber had retailed to him. He was in ecstasy's seventh heaven; and when, Mrs. Matheson having retired pleading a headache, sudden business called Merrilyn's father out and he found himself alone with her, Girt's pulse jumped like a little frightened rabbit.

He never could remember what they talked of, nor what the clock said when he left. But like a bonfire in his mind was the memory of Merrilyn's parting look — of those husky tones, so warm with love and promise when, at last having gotten him to the door, she said: "And you must come back — real soon!"

He did.

Three nights that week he called and each time ate with the Mathesons; and never thought it queer Mother always retired with a headache so early or that business laid such claim on the banker until, about ten o'clock of the fourth night's call, Merrilyn said, blushing prettily:

"Girt — Father's in an awful hole. I — I wonder if you could help him?"

"Why sure!" Girt told her heartily. "You bet I will! — er, that is, leastways, if I can —"

"Oh, you *can!*" she assured him breathlessly. "He has boundless faith in your ability — so have *I,*" she added softly, and brushed his cheek with her fingertips. "You're smart, Girt — you can do *anything!* You might even be *governor* some day." She laughed deliciously at the prospect. "Well, you *might,*" she said more earnestly; "and I could help you, too — you think I'm clever, Girt, don't you?"

"Hell's bells — yes! If I had half your brains —"

"But you *have!*" she exclaimed. "Look at the way you worked Cash Benson! I thought I would faint, I was so scared. That man has the meanest eye! I don't see how you thought at all with him looking at you so ugly! And the clever way you talked him into letting you get that shotgun —"

"Oh, *that!* That was luck," Girt told her blushing. "Cry-*minie*, yes! I expected any second he was goin' to sieve me with that sixgun." He scowled at the memory, then shook thought of Benson away. "What's your ol' man done? Robbed the bank?" he asked facetiously.

Merrilyn Matheson looked at him startled, lips parted, breath hung in her throat. But only for a second; then she laughed. It was a tinkle of chimes; and she said huskily: "How awful, Girt! I thought for a second you meant it. I never can tell when you're joking. Now" — the elves of mischief danced out of her eyes, left them suddenly, gravely, solemn — "do be serious. This means so much to poor Dad."

"Why, sure," Girt said. "What's wrong with him?"

"Well, nothing *really*. But he's always doing so much for other people — I told him he'd get in a jam sometime; and he has. Do you know Uncle Jim Garson?"

She looked, Girt thought, like he'd ought to. But "No," he said, "who is he?"

"He's a rancher — runs a big spread over in Guadalupe County; the HIJ. It's over east of Vaughn, on the Pecos a little bit north of Fort Sumner. And that's just the trouble. It's a good piece off and right now Father can't spare the time to go over and . . ."

But Girt was only half listening. He did want to help, but with Merry so near, so intoxicatingly close to him, about all he could conscientiously concentrate on was *her* — those flower-bright eyes so big and round and childlike, those berry-red tempting lips, the cameo contour of ivory cheeks and the pulse-jumping way her long lashes swept up and down as she blushed prettily under his scrutiny.

"What's he want to go over there for?" he asked, suddenly aware he was expected to say something.

"Well, he doesn't, of course — particularly right now when he's so busy with all these mining deals and all. But Uncle Jim's done Dad a lot of favors — important ones; things that meant the difference between success and failure to Dad when he was working his way up. It wouldn't seem grateful for Dad not to oblige him now when Uncle Jim wants a favor and Dad's in a position to —"

"What's this Garson want him to do?"

Merrilyn frowned sort of thoughtful, like she was trying to shape it up in her mind.

"Dad got a letter from him about a month ago, asking him to send over a bunch of bolts and stuff you use when you're building wagons — freight wagons. Uncle Jim was getting up a caravan to go down into Mexico and bring back a lot of native merchandise to sell at his trading post — you know; hand-made furniture, baskets, tin candlesticks and lanterns and mirrors and rugs and stuff like that. Well, he wanted Dad to send those bolts and things right over, and Dad forgot all about it. And then today he got another letter from Uncle Jim raising the devil about it because Dad had not done it and his freighting outfit was held up and — Oh, I don't know all the details, but he was mad as hops and threw it up to Dad about how he had helped him and all and this was what he got for it. And he said Dad needn't think himself so high and mighty; it was *his* friends that had put the money into Dad's bank to start it and he guessed they could take it out just as quick if he wanted to drop a word to them. And now he wants Dad to send him *immediately* some deeds and stocks and things he's had on deposit and —"

"Well, your father don't have to take 'em to him personal, does he?"

"Well, he ought to. He feels like he owes

Uncle Jim an explanation. And, besides, he thinks he ought to go and try to soothe Uncle Jim down so that all Uncle Jim's friends won't draw their money out. That would put Dad in an awful fix because he's got a lot of money out in investments and might find it hard to get hold of so much money in one lump."

"Well, couldn't he send the stuff over by someone, with a letter or something? I know just the fellow!" Girt said, whacking his thigh. "Good talker, too, my deputy. Yaggy Nettleton!"

Merrilyn's penciled eyebrows climbed excitedly up her forehead. "Not *him!* Not ever Nettleton! Why, he's the Governor's nephew — he hasn't any use for Father *at all!* Dad's been trying to get Governor Axtell out of office — been pulling strings at Washington. Nettleton would never lift a hand —"

"He wouldn't have to know what he was carrying —"

"No," Merrilyn said emphatically. "We can't ask him! Dad might trust *you* to go for him; but not Yaggy Nettleton. And please don't say anything to Mr. Nettleton about this — Dad would never forgive me. Couldn't *you* do it, Girt — for *me?*" she pleaded anxiously. "And it would do you a lot of good with Dad, too."

She affected not to notice how Girt's arm had snuk about her shoulders; sat looking up at him gravely, lower lip caught between the shine of teeth.

Girt said boldly: "Doggone, but you're an eyeful!" and she blushed prettily, lowering her lashes in that devastating way that Girt adored. Girt pulled her to him, and she offered no resistance; but when he would have kissed her she slipped aside.

"We'll have lots of time for that when you get back. . . . Girt — well, just once. But you'll go for me, Girt, won't you?"

So, of course, Girt said he would. He'd have built the doggone wagons, had she asked him!

18

It was all set.

Girt was to leave next morning early; and was just going around to the sheriff's office to give fat Yaggy the law on what was to be which during his absence when, rounding Plain Street's corner onto Hassayamp, he came face to face with a gent whose buck teeth showed in a grin as he hailed joyously: "Hi there, Girt! By jinks, we made it — come through without a scratch!"

Bill Bonney, by grab! and looking mighty prosperous in his forty-dollar hat, checked shirt and cowhide vest. The Kid had on new boots, too — fancy soft-topped Hyer boots equipped with silver spurs, with rowels as big as saucers and jingling all over with danglers. Some of the loot, no doubt, they'd lifted from Alex's store, Girt thought, casting around for something to say.

"You don't look overjoyed to see me," Bonney said with an edge of truculence.

"What's the matter, guy? Ain't we amigos? Didn't you ask me up here?"

Some nerve, Girt thought, after all that had passed between them! — throwing that invite in his teeth, by grab, after the conniving way he had wangled it!

Girt scowled, mind a-churn with resentment. But with the best face he could put on the matter he grumbled, "I'm glad right enough you got through, Bill; but there's a bad feelin' round this town at the moment, an' you being here ain't goin' to help it any —"

"Why, as fer that," the Kid said, "I'll behave like a lamb. An' so will my outfit, too, boy. 'Live an' let live' is my motto," he grinned. "And no one will guess who I am 'less you tell 'em. Just call me 'Mister Williams'," and with a laugh he slapped Girt on the back, just like when they'd punched cows for John Chisum.

But a heap of mud had been washed down the river since those days. Girt took things in at a discount now and he knew the Kid for no kind of guy to play tag with. Bonney was a damn tough monkey and out for all he could get. If only, Girt thought, he hadn't agreed to give the fellow a hideout! But that milk was spined; the Kid was here and regress would oil no sixguns.

"Okay, Bill," he grunted, "but keep yourself out of the limelight. If folks get wise you're here, I'll be expected to do something about it."

"Sure, I savvy." The Kid chuckled. "Come you have to take after me, I'll sure run like a rabbit. But, no joshin', boy, I'm powerful glad to be here — Lincoln has sure enough kicked the lid off. Even John Chisum — the ongrateful hound — has turned on me; every weed-bender in the country is a-yowlin' for my scalp! An' Pat Garrett who used to call himself my friend has offered to ride out an' get me. An' that stinkin' Cattle Association has sicced that butcher, Poe, on me — I tell you, boy, I ain't got a friend in the world! Every man's hands is against me!"

There'd been a time, Girt thought resentfully, when that sort of hogwash had moved him — but not any more, by grab! Bonney was reaping the crop he had sowed; he deserved every bit they could give him — robbing a poor defenseless widow woman just to hang some damn dirt on Jim Dolan! This Kid was a bad one and no mistake; and Girt wished the hell he was out of here.

"Uh — by the way," the Kid said with an

elaborate display of casualness. "That present I give you — still got it?"

"Sure."

"Didn't see you smokin' it. Thought mebbe you'd got tired of it. Got 'er on you?"

About to nod, Girt caught a peculiar gleam in the Kid's blue eyes. "I reckon," he lied, patting pockets, "I must've left it at the office."

"No matter; I just wondered."

Wondering himself, Girt nodded. "Well, you keep out of sight," he said, "an' I'll do the best I can. But remember this — I'm all through bein' shoved, boy. You stay away from Merry Matheson if you expect to stay friends with me!"

Girt started again for the office but once more found himself waylaid. Darinthy-May stopped him this time. "Say — wait," she said; and Girt saw a funny look in her eyes. "What's this I hear about you running errands for Matheson? That straight? Mean to say you've joined the Boot-Lickers Club an' are playin' cat's-paw for that vinegarroon?"

"I — er — well," Girt stammered, cheeks burning under that accusing stare, "I've agreed to help him out a little. He's in a hole an' —"

"A hole, eh?" she snapped with a cutting scorn. "Why, you yammerin' nitwit! That hole ain't *nothin'* to the hole *you'll* be in!" And she went flouncing off in a fury.

"I'll be a rhino's uncle!" scowled Girt after watching her out of sight. "Now what in seven devils ails *her?* Hole! Boot-Lickers Club!" He snorted. "If all the janes was like her, by grab, it would sure be a hard day for matrimony!" And, still muttering to himself, he went stamping over to the office.

Yaggy, the governor's nephew, was pawing things over like he'd lost something, and puffing like a walrus. "What's the matter?" asked Girt. "Mislaid your false teeth?"

"Whew — pick me up, Gerty!" the chief deputy wheezed, wiping the sweat from his triple chins. "Of all the crazy-fool stunts I ever heard — Who'd wanta burgle a sheriff's office? An' what the hell was they after?"

He stared at Sasabe owlishly; and Girt blinked back at him baffled. "Are you tellin' me somebody *robbed* this joint?"

"They sure made a pass at it, anyhow! Here — help me look; I wanta know what that bird was after."

"Bird? What kinda bird?"

"Sawed-off squirt with a set of buck teeth — I didn't get a good look at him. He was gettin' out the window jest as I was comin' in the door — I'd been over to the Broken Stopper for a cup of tea. He musta heard me comin'; halfway through that winder by the time I got the door open."

A little bee got to buzzing in Girt's bonnet as he helped Yaggy comb the place over; it was not a full-fledged notion but just a sort of vague idea that he kept to himself to think over.

They turned the office upside down but nothing appeared to be missing. Yaggy eyed Girt with a baffled look and scowled at the window belligerently. "Damnedest thing I ever heard of — 'f I hadn't seen the whippoorwill, I'd of swore I had a pipe dream."

"What kind of rig was he wearin' — Levis, store pants, chaps?"

"Durned if I know — I never noticed," Yaggy said; "except he had on fancy Hyer boots. I lamped one of them as he lugged it across the sill over there."

Girt nodded very thoughtful-like and abruptly changed the subject. "I'll be leavin' town for a bit in the morning — takin' a pasear over into Guadalupe County. Matter of business —"

"Whose business? Matheson's?" Yaggy's tone was sharp.

So was the look Girt snapped at him. "By gee, a guy can't take a breath around here without the whole town knows it!" he complained in exasperation. "What if I am goin' for Matheson? You know any law against it?"

But Yaggy took no offense at his manner. "I ain't one fer givin' advice, boy; but I been around here quite a spell — outlasted two-three sheriffs, I have, an' it's been my observation —"

"Horse feathers!" Girt snapped arrogantly, after the manner of the Kid. "You tryin' to tell me how to run my business?"

"No," Yaggy said; "only was I you, I'd quit nobbin' round with them Mathesons. Nothin' personal in that," he added hastily, ducking the look in Girt's eye. "It's jest that Clay's politics is skiddin' him down for a crack-up an' there ain't no sense you gettin' your head cracked too."

"You tend to your knittin' an' never mind me," Girt growled, "or there'll be a new deputy around this office! By grab," he snarled with his hackles up, "you keep your jaw off'n my business, boy, or I'll put it in a plaster!"

And, with a final hard look, he stamped

208

out of the place in a passion.

He left town early and was halfway to Vaughn before he recollected last night's burglary. And the bee that had buzzed in his bonnet. Pulling up with an oath, he dragged Bonney's pipe from his pocket; sat scowling down at it truculently.

There was nothing unusual about it. Just an ordinary native briar, hand carved, with a thick, curved stem and a squat-shaped chunky bowl. Not a handsome hod from any angle, nor did it have an especially good taste; but the Kid had given it to him before they got on the outs, so he'd kept it and smoked the thing anyway. He'd half a notion to heave it off in the brush. "If it wasn't for that robbery —"

That was just it. He'd have bet his boots the man Yaggy'd seen getting out of the window was smiling Bill Bonney in person! "I reckon," Girt had said, "I must of left it at the office"; and pronto the office was raided.

There was a connection there if he could get it — but before he did, he spied a dust coming down the road; a big dust that drove thoughts of Bonney from his mind.

Girt rammed the pipe in his pocket with an oath as he recognized the oncoming riders — Dad Peppin with a ten-man posse, and every jack armed to the teeth!

"What the hell!" Peppin said, with his eye roving over Girt's pack horse. "Goin' prospectin'? What you done — quit your sheriff's job?"

"The answer's *no* to both questions. Just takin' a pasear over to the Pecos on business," Girt said, wondering what in the devil they were doing here. "Ain't you kind of out of your bailiwick, Peppin?"

"We was headin' for Broken Stirrup — got a hot tip on Bonney." The Lincoln sheriff eyed Girt oddly. "Didn't you know he was in your neighborhood?"

"Is that so?" Girt demanded, scowling. "Judas Priest! You tryin' to load me?"

"Load, hell!" said Peppin roughly. "He's here all right — we tracked 'im more'n halfway. An' we ain't *all* that's on that sidewinder's trail, either; not by a damn sight! Remember how a bunch stopped the Overland Flyer a couple months back south of Cambray? It was Bonney's bunch, we've found out — railroad's got dicks out huntin' him. An' the cattle crowd's got men lookin' up his pedigree likewise. I tell you, boy, that vinegarroon's about reached the end of his rope."

Girt rasped his jaw uneasily. "Well, thanks for the information, Sheriff, an' for all your trouble —"

"Beg pardon?" Peppin's eye showed frost. "We didn't take this ride just to tell you Bonney was here; we've come along to help you *get* him —"

"That's mighty good of you, Peppin," Girt said. "But if Bonney's around here, I can handle him without no help —"

"No help?" said Peppin blankly; and there were growls from the possemen back of him. "See here, boy; that talk is plumb foolish! Ain't I been after that chipmunk for months an' never yet got my hands on him?"

"Yeah — but you used the wrong technique," Girt informed him, "an' you don't know Bill Bonney like *I* do. If he starts loosin' his didoes around here —"

"Well, you can take it from me, he will," Peppin snapped. "You may be slicker'n greased splatters, but no damn-fool boy —"

"Shucks," Girt broke in with a chuckle. "I've known Bill from way back yonder. His rep's made you fellows too cautious — that's how he keeps the game goin'. I used to think myself he had more guts than you could rightly hang to a fencepost. But I dunno; he's done a mort of things that took no more nerve than I've got —"

"Are you allowin' to tell us you're

refusin' my offer of aid?"

"I wasn't aimin' to put it so blunt," Girt observed, looking over the posse. "But heck," he scoffed, "after all, who killed Goliath with a slingshot? Just a damn-fool kid like me, wasn't it? Don't you fret yourself about *me*, Sheriff; I can handle three like the Kid, with both hands tied and one eye shut."

For a long second Peppin stared grimly. "Goin' to scorch him all by yourself, eh?"

"You watch my smoke," Girt promised.

"Yeah — I'll be watchin'," Peppin told him darkly. "An' so will the rest of this county!"

Well, he was out on a limb now, right enough, Girt thought, scowling after the posse. Peppin's thoughts had been plainer than paint and Girt cursed the old coot pretty bitter. But curses, he thought, wouldn't help him now any more than berating his luck. The fat was in the fire, and the fault was his for promising the Kid shelter in the first place. Bonney, miles ahead of the game like always, had played him for a sucker.

"Okay!" Girt told himself steamily. "Mebbe I *am* a sucker; but you watch out, Bill Bonney, or we'll see who gets to laugh last!"

★ ★ ★

By dint of considerable questions Girt finally found the outfit; but the hard stares he got at each asking brought him to the Garson spread in a mood that was downright thoughtful. Nor did this mood ease off any when from a hilltop he looked the place over. It was an efficient enough looking outfit, all right, if it wasn't just what he'd been picturing. It was the HIJ's location that, with the stares, had got Girt to wondering. Tucked away, it was, like a needle in a haystack; and manned by a large, tough crew. Too large a crew for its size, Girt thought, and squinted around uneasily as he pulled to a stop by the porch. He was glad he'd had the foresight to leave his badge pinned in his pocket.

A man eased out of the bunkhouse with a rifle in the crook of his arm. "Huntin' somethin'?"

"Huntin' Garson," Girt answered, ignoring his tone and the man he saw peering from the harness shed. "Is he anyplace around?"

The rifle-toter was eyeing Girt's pack horse. "What you wantin' him for?"

"I'll tell him that when I see him. You his private secretary?"

The man scowled, then leered knowingly. "Quite a card, boy, ain't you? Happens I'm Garson's range boss. There ain't a thing you can do for him, so if you're another of them travelin' underwear merchants, you can turn right around an' —"

"Hell, I'm king of the Banziboo Islands!" Girt told him and, sliding out of his saddle, went up and banged on the door.

He could feel the fellow's hard scrutiny rubbing against his back; and the prying eyes of the guy in the harness shed made him wonder what he'd got into. But having come this far, he aimed to see Matheson's benefactor or know the reason why. All the same, he was glad the piece of tin he packed was safe hid out of sight.

Heavy boots sent echoes down an inside hall and then the door was flung open. "Another yardstick salesman, boss," called the man by the bunkhouse meaningly.

Girt's quick appraisal of Garson did not compliment the impression of the man he had gathered from Merrilyn's talk of him. "Uncle Jim" was hardly the sort of hombre anyone would apply that title to — so far as looks went anyhow. He was a chunky, block-shaped man with a high flat face and copper cheeks and a black patch over one eye. "You lookin' fer me?" he grunted; and the good eye swept Girt like a spotlight.

"If your name's Garson," Girt nodded. "Clay Matheson sent me over."

"Oh!" Garson said, and his manner changed completely. He shoved open the screen. "Come on in — glad to see any friend of Matheson's. Ain't seen Clay for quite a spell an' — here! Step right in here," he said, and led the way into a low-beamed room that evidently served for an office. It was cluttered with oddments of gear, an old saddle or two, and had a case of stacked rifles in one corner. He shoved some junk from a chair and, getting out a bottle, took a seat on the edge of his desk. "How is Clay, anyhow? Did he get my note?" he asked, grinning.

"I reckon so," Girt told him. "He was sure in a lather for me to get here. I —"

"Did he send that stuff — them papers an' bolts?"

"Well, no-o," Girt lied; and Garson's look of eagerness fell away like an undermined cutbank. His cheeks took on a bloated, poisonous cast and the light in his eye turned ugly. "Well, that sneakin', double-crossin' —"

"Now wait!" Girt gulped, holding up a hand. "Take it easy, old-timer, till I tell you. He's sendin' it down right enough, just like he promised; only he's bringin' it

215

down himself an' —"

"Bringin' it himself!" Garson shouted. "Is the goddam fool hog-crazy? I told —"

"Well, *I* told him, too," declared Girt, scowling hard as Garson. "But you know Clay — too bullheaded to listen. He allowed he'd bring it down himself an', after all, I'm only workin' for him. He said I should come on ahead an' give you the word he was comin' an' —"

"What the hell you got that pack horse for?" demanded Garson supsiciously. "If you ain't brought the stuff —"

Girt said scornfully: "That was Clay's idea. He said if anyone happened to stop me —"

Garson raved, called the banker every name on the calendar. "That's always been his trouble!" he stormed. "So goddam cautious you kin taste it! One of these days —"

"That's what I told him," Girt said, thinking fast.

"But —"

"When's he coming?" Garson growled thickly.

"Said to tell you he'd be down in a day or two. Got a couple of details still to arrange —"

"Details!" Garson cursed; and still was cursing when Girt eased out of the picture.

But not until he was back inside his own bailiwick did Girt draw a full breath or finally quit staring across his shoulder. Then he stopped and mopped his face and growled a relieved "Cry-*minie!*"

It had been pretty close — pretty dog-goned close, and he was a long ways from being sure yet; but it looked mighty like Darinthy-May had been right and he'd nearly been played for a sucker. "Danged quick work all around," he muttered. "An' if gettin' me out of town is any good to Matheson, he sure as hell is welcome —but who'd have thought a nice lookin' girl like Merry would try to put the skids under a lawman?" And with a final bitter oath, he roweled his bronc in a passion and went storming into the county seat like the tail of a Kansas twister.

19

Yaggy looked up with a start as Girt
whipped into the Honky-Donk Hash House
at twenty-three minutes past eleven — p.m.
There were smoldering lights in the sheriff's
blue eyes and the look on his cheeks was a
warning. "Well!" he said; and Yaggy grinned
at him foolishly. "Wasn't expectin' you back
before mornin' —"

"You needn't tell me!" Girt snapped. "I
got eyes in my head!" and he chucked
Yaggy's look back nastily. "So this here's
the way you spend your time when I take a
pasear out of town! By grab, you keep
away from my girl or I'll make you hard to
lay hands on!"

Yaggy's jaw dropped an inch per chin.
He stared at the sheriff bug-eyed. "Your
girl? I thought you said —"

"Never mind what you thought! This
here is *my* girl an' —"

"*Your girl!*" Darinthy-May laughed scornfully. "Not so you could notice it! When I
take on a husband, *boy,* I'll find something

brighter than *you!*"

"I'm bright enough," Girt snapped; "I just ain't been gettin' no breaks. But things'll be different hereafter! Pick all the husbands you want an' I'll plant 'em. As fer *you*" — he scowled at Yaggy — "you git over to the office pronto — I got a lot to say to you!"

"You mean *now?*" Yaggy wheezed.

"*Right* now — an' never mind sayin' good night!"

"Say!" Darinthy-May stormed. "You can't order my customers out of here —"

"I have! an' by grab he'll stay out! Now keep your shirt on, Darinthy — I've got a lot to say to you, too. But it'll take more time'n I've got right now; an' anyhow I got to get a ring first. *But I'll be back* — you pick out the day." And, leaving her staring after him, for once too astonished for a comeback, Girt followed fat Yaggy out.

But once outside a new thought struck him. "You go on over to the office," he told the chief deputy, "an' stay right there till I get there."

Bonney had been lodging at Mother Humphrey's place; and it took just three minutes. The Kid, for a wonder, was there and up. Girt found him playing cards with a couple of other guests and beckoned him out peremptorily. "Where's the rest of your crowd?" he demanded soon as the door closed back of them.

"They're around someplace, I guess — why?"

"Just this," Girt said. "I'm onto your little game, my friend; an' it's out — plumb out! Do you get me?"

Bonney scowled up at him thoughtfully. "I'm afraid I don't — what game are you talkin' about?"

That line might have fooled Girt once, but he'd got the wool off his eyes. "Never mind," he shrugged. "Just gather up your playmates an' hit the trail out of here —"

"What? Orderin' me out? Why, I thought you an' me was friends, boy —"

"We was — when we worked for Chisum. But them days is gone an' I'm all through bein' played for a sucker. I'm warnin' you, Bill — an' the last time, too; get out if you want to keep healthy."

Bonney stared down at his hands. In the light from the living room window Girt could see his expression was wistful. But he'd sampled the Kid's acting before and had been monkey-on-a-stick all he aimed to. "I mean it," he said grimly. "Take your gang out of Torrance an' stay out."

The Kid shook his head with a sigh.

"Okay, boy — if you wish it." He seemed to scan something in his mind. He said then, softly, reproachfully: "I thought I could count on *you*, boy; thought you'd do to ride the river with. . . ." He paused expectantly; but when Girt didn't bite, he snarled bitterly: "Every man's hand is against me — you'd think I was a goddam wolf or somethin'! An' all I ask is to be left alone, to live my life like other guys. I don't want to fight — to be all the time shootin' an' killin'! I —"

"Yeah," Girt said. "All who believe that go stand on their head!"

The Kid went stiff, went motionless. His face set like a mask. Only the eyes were alive; and they were wicked.

"You callin' me a liar, boy?"

"You're golrammed tootin'!" Girt gritted, and struck as the Kid reached for leather.

Back in the sheriff's office, Yaggy Nettleton went taut at the sound of hurried boots. His heavy-set frame arched forward in something that was very like a crouch and the stubby fingers of a hamlike fist splayed out above his holster. His eyes showed coldly alert and he moved mighty soft for a fat man as he backed away from the desk.

Then the door swept open. A coatless, hatless man broke in, panting, disheveled; eyes rolling wildly in the grip of some vast excitement.

Yaggy came out of his crouch, grabbed the fellow — *hard*. "What's up, Handers? For God's sake spill it quick."

The follow's eyes rolled again; but Yaggy's urgent tone had its influence. Handers gulped, grabbed for breath and caught it. "The bank," he gasped. "The Broken Stirrup National. They've blown the vault."

"*Who* has?"

Handers looked startled. "Bandit's! Gutted it — left it clean as a baby's leg."

The expression of Yaggy's eyes grew intently thoughtful; calculating. The mark of some secret humor briefly touched his cheeks as he left go of Handers' shoulder and stepped back to lounge one hip against the desk. "You've seen Matheson?"

"Not — not Matheson —"

"Crandell, the teller, then?"

"I ain't seen no one," Handers declared, "except the bunch that rushed over there with me when we heard the door let go." To Yaggy's probing glance he said: "We was over to the Broken Stopper — right next door, you know — me an' Haines an'

Jastro — couple of other gents. Harry'd just poured us out a nightcap when '*Wham!*' — it sounded like hell had blown the boiler up. 'The bank!' Haines said; an' we all went larrupin' over. An' sure enough! It *was!* Front of the vault was blowed clean 'cross the place — layin' front of the door, it was, an' —"

"Let's go," Yaggy said grimly, shoving Handers toward the door. "We'd better get Crandell over there right away an' check up on how much is —"

"Where's the sheriff?"

"He'll be along." Nettleton's drawl was more pronounced. The look in his eye was gloating.

The force of Girt's blow rocked the Kid straight back on his boot-heels. He lost his balance — stumbled. Girt kicked the gun from his hand.

Against the cedar-post fence the Kid crouched, face murderous, slitted eyes blazing. With a sudden quick shift he sprang, lunging sideways after the gun. But Girt stamped a boot on it; met the Kid's rush with a hook brought up from his bootstraps.

The fence checked Bonney's form again, spread-eagled it. He hung there, wild-eyed, gasping; clawing whistling breath through the white clenched teeth disclosed by his curled-back lips.

"Better call it quits while you're able," Girt gritted. "Call it quits or I'll bust you in two."

"You stinkin' bustard! I'll make you rue this if it's the last thing I ever do!" Bonney swore in a burst of vile invective. "You double-crossin' hound! You got me up here with the promise of a hideout —"

"Never mind all that," Girt told him. "I been played for a sucker enough! You claimed you wanted a hideout — not a headquarters for more of your deviltry! You couldn't play square if you tried to!"

They glared at each other, those two, with the light from Maw Humphrey's windows boldly picking out their faces. They weren't four feet apart and Girt could see the wicked fury churning the depths of the Kid's slimmed stare. There'd been a time when a look like that from the Kid would have shriveled him — but not any more; he had the Kid's number how, knew Bonney for what he was. A mad-dog killer — just what Sheriff Brady had called him. If he could have got his hand on a gun right then, he'd have sieved Girt without compunction.

The tautness went out of the Kid's wiry figure; he wiped the blood from his chin and Girt saw how the raised hand was shaking. But he felt no pity for him now; all that was gone, wiped out by the Kid's intended treachery. "Get your gang," Girt told him scornfully, "an' hit the trail *muy pronto.* If you cross my tracks again I'm goin' to jail you."

Vindictively Bonney cursed him, named him every foul thing he could think of; and Girt took it all in calmly with a cold grin curving his lips. When lack of breath brought the Kid to a pause, he said wryly: "I blush to think I ever tried to make myself like you; but it's a fact, Bill. I used to think you was some pumpkins; tried to copy all your slick little ways an' thought I was a scissor-bill 'cause I couldn't be as tough as you were. Cry-*minie!* what a yap I was! But I'm all cured now an' you better drag tail out of here while I'm still feelin' a little generous."

The Kid said thickly: "If I could get my hands on a gun —"

"Yeah — sure!" Girt mocked. "You're brave as hell when you got a gun! One chance in a million's all you ask — that's your brag, boy, ain't it?" Girt eyed him, blue glance jeering. "Here it is," he said, and threw his pistol into the road. "Go ahead now, bravo — cut your wolf loose!"

But the Kid just stood there, glaring.

Girt walked over and picked up his gun, jammed the Colt into leather contemptuously. "Same breed as Benson!" he observed with high scorn; "just a chicken-stealin' coyote! If you're in this county come dawn, by grab, I'm handin' you over to Peppin!" And without another glance at the Kid, he stamped off into the darkness.

20

On his way to the office Girt passed the bank and, at sight of the muttering, gesticulating crowd before it, a sour smile crossed his lips. But there was no smile on them when he crossed the street and entered, shoving men off his elbows. Yaggy was there and Crandell, the teller; and Crandell's cheeks were haggard. "I don't know," he kept muttering. "I don't know, I tell you." He said dazedly, "Everything was all right when I left —"

"Let's hear the story," Girt said crisply.

This being Saturday night, the teller said, the bank had not closed till nine-thirty. He himself had been the last to leave; about quarter to eleven that had been, he said. "Everything was all right then. This robbery must have taken place since —"

"Sure," remarked Yaggy. "Handers, here, and some of the boys heard the door go — about eleven-forty, Handers says; he was havin' a drink in the Stopper."

Girt nodded; said, "Clear these guys out of here, Yaggy." And when Yaggy had done so and bolted the broken front door that had been ripped nearly apart by the blast, Girt asked Crandell calmly: "How much did they get? Checked up yet?"

Crandell nodded, passing a hand across his eyes. He said drearily: "One hundred thousand in gold."

Head tipped back, with his tongue at the edge of his lips, Girt eyed him knowingly. "They didn't touch the silver," Yaggy said, looking sharply at Girt.

"No, I didn't reckon so — too much weight to bother with. Grabbed a pile of deeds, securities an' things though, didn't they?"

The teller looked startled. "Why — I don't know. I hadn't —"

"Well, you go take a look," Girt said, and took Yaggy over beside what was left of the grillwork. With one hand draping his gun-butt he said: "You an' me'll have that talk now, fellow. What sort of game you playin' here? Who you workin' for? Bonney or Benson?"

Yaggy said, "Huh?" and his jaw dropped down a full inch.

"Never mind the act," Girt snapped. "This whole town's been tryin' to play me for a sucker, but my sucker days is over, boy — you talk, an' talk dang quick!"

Looking completely baffled, Yaggy mopped his triple chins; but Girt's gun, shoved in his paunch, changed the look in the deputy's eyes pronto. "Talk," Girt grunted; "an' never mind that bull about bein' the governor's nephew —"

"Who says I ain't his nephew?"

"Axtell says so — says he ain't got no nephew! I wired him this evenin' from Vaughn. Now you talk, boy, an' make it good or I'll put you with the rest of the bull-throwers!"

"Oh-ho!" Yaggy grinned. "The boy's woke up —"

"You're golrammed right he has! You better make this good!"

Eyes twinkling, Yaggy flipped back his vest. "Okay, pardner; look 'er over," he said, and chuckled at Girt's surprised oath. "You're lookin' at the only two-badge lawman," he grinned, "this side of the Mississippi."

"Deputy marshal!" Girt growled, and swore in disgust. "I thought you was one of the crooks!"

Crandell came catfooting back with a drawn, worried look in his eye. He fiddled with his watch chain nervously and the look he gave them was bewildered. "I can't think how you guessed it, Sheriff — but you were right; there's a bunch of stocks and deeds gone —"

"Sure. Well, you come along with us," Girt said, "an' mebbe you can think what's happened to 'em."

Crandell cast a helpless look about. "Don't you think I'd ought to stay here an' —"

"Nothin' of the kind," ruled Girt. "You're goin' to occupy a nice clean cell in the Broken Stirrup jail where we'll know where to find you when we want you!" And, before the white-faced teller could collect his scattered wits, Girt had deftly removed the pistol from his pocket.

With a firm grip on Crandell's shoulder, he said to Yaggy's startled look: "Yeah — this is one of 'em; an' if he wants to squeal, it may save us a little trouble. But whether he does or not, I expect I can piece out the story."

"You mean to say he was in on this thing?"

"Up to his neck in it!" Girt grunted. "Didn't you hear him admit he was the last guy out of the bank tonight? That safe was blown by dynamite — an inside job made to look like a raid by use of a long fuse or something. That vault was looted before they blew the door off —"

"Whew! Leave me up for air, boy. Did you figure this all by deduction?"

"Hell, no," Girt said with a guffaw. "I've got the loot hid in our office!"

21

"In the office!" Yaggy cried; and, in his amazement, shoved an entire pack of gum in his mouth without peeling off the papers. "My gosh, boy! Slow 'er up a little — you're too danged fast for a fat man!" There was an open admiration in his stare though as he said: "How the heck did you get a-holt of it? And how come there ain't no fireworks? If I'd stole all that jack, by jinks I'd not get parted from it without one bird of a row —"

"They ain't missed it yet," Girt chuckled; and told the government man how he'd started getting suspicious of Matheson soon as he'd brought Merrilyn back from Bonney's hideout. "He didn't ring true, heapin' all them favors on a plain cow ranny like me; an' when I kep' gettin' invites back, I knew they had somethin' cookin'. Oh, I'll admit," Girt said, grinning sheepishly, "I enjoyed all them attentions; but away down at the back of my mind —"

"Hell," chuckled in Crandell nastily, "you was takin' it hook, line an' sinker!"

Girt flicked the teller a cold hard look. "And what do *you* know about it? Were you hep to that part, too?"

"You think you're the greatest law-giver since Moses," Crandell sneered; "but you got a heap to learn, boy. That jane's goin' to be my wife —" He broke off, scowling, as Girt flipped a wink at Yaggy.

"You may be right," Girt grinned; "but not unless she likes wearin' ear muffs. They say it gets damn cold in Siberia"; and ignoring the fellow then, he went on to explain that, though he had agreed to take some bolts and papers over to Uncle Jim Garson on the Pecos, he'd been far less taken in than they'd thought him. "Of course, I owe a heap to D'rinthy-May — she's got a head on her shoulders, that girl has! She got hold of me last night just before I quit town and sure give me something to think about. Puttin' one thing an' another together, by the time I got to Garson's place I was ready to suspect my own grandmother. An' was that 'Uncle Jim' guy a beauty! Everybody I asked where Garson's spread was looked me over like I was batty," Girt said; "but when I asked where the HIJ was they could tell me with their eyes shut — only for that I mightn't of caught on. Merry'd ought to've told me his right name in the first place, 'cause by the time I got to see him I was pretty damn suspicious —"

"You mean that 'Uncle Jim' build-up," Yaggy said, "was a blind?"

"It was somethin', all right. D'you know who that guy was?"

"Who was he?"

"The King of Tularosa — *Pat Coghlin!*" Girt said; and Yaggy swore.

"You sure of that?"

"You bet! I seen his picture in a paper once; might not have recollected if I hadn't been suspicious — but he's Coghlin right enough," Girt declared, and Yaggy looked mighty thoughtful.

"Chisum," he said, "swears Coghlin's been buying his Jingle-Bob cattle fast as the Kid can steal them. From what you tell me, that place of his on the Pecos is an ideal layout for —"

"It's ideal, all right; an' they're all settin' round with rifles. It would take the U.S. Army," Girt growled, "to blast 'em out of there!"

Yaggy was turning something over in his mind. He said abruptly: "You know the Kid's in town, don't you?"

"Ah. . . . *Is* he?" Girt asked; and flushed under the marshal's sharp scrutiny. "That how come you're in this? You here after Bill Bonney?"

"I'm after Bonney, sure," Yaggy said; "but I'd like to bag the whole crew of 'em — the Kid, Matheson —"

"Cry-*minie!*" Girt yelled. "That reminds me! I better get after that buck pronto, before he gets the wind up and hops it! The golrammed woodchuck was figurin' to make me the goat on that bank-guttin' — bet you he's all fixed with witnesses ready to swear they seen me gettin' out of town with a pack horse all bogged down under that hundred thousan' —"

"Hold on," Yaggy said, grabbing hold of him. "Don't go off half-cocked, Sheriff! You left here this mornin'; that vault was blown tonight!"

"Yeah-that's right," Girt muttered, scowling. "Must of changed their plans. . . ." He stared suspiciously at Crandell. "What was the big idea?"

But Crandell was all through talking. No threat of Girt's could move him. Girt turned to Yaggy suddenly. "By grab! D'you suppose Coghlin could of wired Matheson?"

"He might have — but in that case, why go on with it? Why pull that phony robbery tonight?"

"Yeah, that's so, too. Hey, wait!" Girt cried excitedly. "Mebbe he was fixing to put it on the *Kid* — mebbe Coghlin *did* wire him; he was pretty dang sore when I left him! Mebbe he wired, raising hell —"

"You're right!" Yaggy said, eyes narrowing. "That clicks all around. Coghlin, sore, wires Matheson; Matheson, suspicious, decides to stage his fake raid later an' dump the blame on Bonney — an' he might, at that, bein' peeved about what you told him concernin' the Kid's designs on his daughter. . . . He'd know Bonney was here, right enough; they been workin' hand-in-glove on this rustlin'. Matheson's been helpin' Coghlin dispose of those worked-over brands; leastways, we *think* he has. That's what they sent me up here for, to check up on Matheson's end of it. There's just one thing puzzles me," Yaggy grumbled. "How was he expectin' to get around your turnin' up with the loot?"

They eyed each other, scowling. "You've took a look at that sack of bolts, haven't you?" Yaggy asked sharply.

Girt shook his head. "I figured —"

"Come on," Yaggy muttered grimly. "We better get this bird in the cage and start checkin' that stuff over pronto!"

"Hadn't we better collect Matheson —"

"You can grab him anytime. We can get him when we go after Bonney; that loot's the important thing right now!"

But Girt, uneasily conscious of his error in warning Bonney to beat it, said determinedly: "You can handle Crandell an' you don't need me to count that gold — you'll find it in the closet under my extra saddle. I'm goin' after Matheson!" And he was off before Yaggy could protest.

Having warned the Kid out of the county, Girt dared not risk losing Matheson too. That would leave the law with nothing but a conniving teller to show for its efforts, while all the Big Knobs got away. Anyhow, he owed Matheson something on his own hook. "I'll learn him to try playin' me for a sucker!" Girt scowled, and banged his fist on the door like a judgment.

Mrs. Matheson stuck her head from an upstairs window. "That you, Clay? Where's your key at *this* time?" she called huffily.

But Girt was not to be taken in by such wiles. "Sheriff Sasabe talkin'," he told her. "Tell Matheson to come down here pronto — his bank's been robbed. I wanta see him!"

"So do *I*, if it comes to that! What's this

you say about the bank being robbed?"

Girt told her. "Now cut out the funny stuff," he said sternly, "an' tell him to get down here *muy pronto* —"

"He's not home, I told you!" Mrs. Matheson shrilled, and banged down her window maliciously.

"You open this door or I'll bust it!"

She opened the window reluctantly. "You don't have to tell the whole neighborhood! Have you got a search warrant?"

"Sure I got a warrant!" Girt hauled back his boot; and Mrs. Matheson came down hurriedly. "You're wasting your time," she snapped, letting him in.

But Girt looked anyway; and when, finally convinced, he found her watching him vindictively, he said rudely: "Where's that slick-talkin' daughter of yours?"

"She's not at home, either. She's spending the night with a friend —"

"Friend's name?" Girt demanded peremptorily. And when, acidulously, she told him, he hurried off to the address. But the friend knew nothing of Merrilyn's visit. "She hasn't been here," they told him, and Girt left them staring pop-eyed at his fluent command of mule language.

He was still frothing when he came stamping into the office. Yaggy looked up at him oddly. "Where'd you say you left them bolts?"

"Right there in the closet —"

"Well, they ain't there now," Yaggy told him.

22

"Ain't there!" yelled Girt.

"Go squint for yourself," Yaggy muttered, dropping into a chair disgustedly. Then, when Girt reappeared glaring steamily: "Reckon that dang banker's cut stick, too, eh?"

Girt's description of Matheson came forth in terms his family would have been ashamed of. "An' that fancy-talkin' filly's jumped the fence, likewise!" he snarled savagely.

"Then it's a lead-pipe cinch," Yaggy grumbled, "that the Kid has flitted also —"

"Mean to say Merry'd go rampin' off with that whippoorwill after all the trouble I taken to pry her loose from him?"

"She didn't never ask you to, did she?"

With an oath Girt grabbed up his Greener, heading for the door.

"Here — hold on! Where you off to?" Yaggy panted, hoisting himself from Girt's chair.

"I'm goin' to —"

"Now hold on — we got to figure this out first," Yaggy muttered. "Who you reckon come in here an' got that loot? Bonney? Matheson? Reckon one of 'em could of seen you come back to town?"

Some of the fierceness washed from Girt's features. Again he was regretting that visit he'd impulsively paid Bill Bonney. If the Kid *was* in on that bank deal it would have been just like him to have stopped by here on his way out of town and carried off that gold with him! Without mentioning the visit, he said as much to Yaggy.

"Oh, he'd grab it right enough if he knew it was here," Yaggy nodded. "But the question is, did he know? Why not Matheson? Seems to me *he'd* be the most likely — special if Coghlin wired him. If it had been me, I'd have cached that loot out of town someplace —"

"Call me a yap and be done with it!"

"Sho'; now don't git frothy, boy. We all make mistakes. To err is —"

"Hell!" exclaimed Girt suddenly. "I almost forgot —" He brought Bonney's pipe from his pocket, held it out toward the marshal.

"What's the vast idea?" said Yaggy staring. "I don't wanta smoke your pipe —"

241

"This here," Girt said, "is a present the Kid gave me down at Lincoln. You recollect that burglary you was jawin' about last' night? Well, I got a hunch it was Bonney, that this pipe is what he was after!"

"Mean to say he'd raid a place jest to git a secon'-hand hod?"

"You keep it anyhow," Girt urged. "Unless I miss my guess it's got those jewels Bonney lifted from the mail coach of the Overland Flyer —"

"What!" gagged Yaggy, grabbing it. "You loadin' me, boy?"

"Bust it open!"

"Not on your tintype," the marshal said, gingerly buttoning it into his pocket. "I'll get it off to Santa Fe first thing in the mornin' — an' if you're right, you got a reward comin', mister, that'll make your eyes bug out! I *hope* you're right; be a feather in our caps an' we're gonna need all we can get, boy, if we mess this up any worser."

He stared at Girt morosely. "What you reckon we better do?"

"I dunno. If I was sure the Kid was in on this —"

"You can take my word he's in it someplace," Yaggy declared emphatically. "With all that mazuma floating round, don't think a guy of his talents is goin' to be curled up takin' a nap!"

"Yeah, it don't seem hardly likely." Girt berated himself for being the cause of Bonney's departure. Then an idea struck him. "Say! Supposin' he hasn't cleared out yet? You got any notion where he's been stayin'?"

"Sure — Mother Humphrey's. Only reason I haven't jumped him sooner is I wanted to bag the whole crew. Bowdre's around here someplace, an' Doc Scurlock an' Middleton an' mebbe two-three others. But it wasn't them so much I was after as Matheson. There's rewards out for them fellers; but Matheson's been too slick — covered his tracks too careful. Way I seen it, it was get him now or —"

"C'mon," Girt said, picking up his shotgun. "Let's go call on Maw Humphrey."

Yaggy said: "Wait'll I blow out the light —"

But somebody blew it out for him. Girt, yanking open the door, felt something whistle past his ear. The light went out in a tinkle of glass as a rifle cracked out yonder.

23

"Gol darn!" cursed Yaggy wickedly.

But Girt wasn't saying anything; he was moving, cat-footing across the warped planking — long, smooth, rhythmic strides that were taking him into that outside darkness while his slimmed eyes raked the banked shadows with a fury that knew but one white-hot desire — that the bushwhacker might try his luck again.

And then, just as he was about to give up hope, the tag-end of his roving glance picked up a blur of movement. It came from a pole corral catty-cornered across the road; and Girt, crouching low above his Greener, hurled himself across the open with a recklessness that would have surprised him in a saner moment. But he was not thinking of safety now — there was no room in his mind for caution; he knew but that one fierce desire, to come to grips with the cowardly skunk who had levered that shot from the darkness — to feel the impact of his knuckles grinding skin from bone.

He heard the wheezed panting of Yaggy's breath behind him; and then, abrupfly, from the slatted shadows of the pole enclosure flame burst again and the *bang! bang! bang!* of a high-powered rifle drove echoes crashing off the building fronts; and as the gun went still, the thump of running boots rose up from the dusty earth and Girt veered sharply to cut the fellow off.

He was making for the blacksmith's shack; Girt emptied the shotgun viciously, spraying the murk with lead. Without pausing, he thumbed a fresh load into the sawed-off barrels and veered again to beat the bushwhacker to the shack's far side — rounded it and crashed full tilt into a crouched figure diving from its shadows.

They went down in a flailing tangle. Girt lost his Greener and slugged with both fists in an effort to batter the man into submission or keep him busy till Yaggy came up.

But the man lashed back at him, cursing; raked a spurred boot down Girt's leg with a force that nearly curled him up with the pain of it. But if the man was desperate, so was Girt; and he was mad clean through. Groaning through clenched teeth, he rolled clear, came to a knee and, as the man came off the ground, tore into him with a fury that put him back down on his shoulders.

Girt tried for a hammerlock, but the man wriggled clear and then they were up again, slugging, battering, lunging — fighting with a recklessness that took no account of hurts. The drive of a sudden rush sent Girt backwards, staggering. But he kept his feet. Maddened, panting, growling, the fellow closed, swung wildly. Ducking, Girt planted his feet. The man swung again and again Girt ducked and then, as that wild swing carried the big fellow forward, Girt came up with a hook that packed every last grim ounce of his weight.

Caught off balance, that lifting fist took the man at the base of the jaw. The knees buckled under him, dropped him backward in a moveless, outsprawled heap.

Yaggy came up, wheezing.

"Grab a leg!" Girt gritted wickedly, and reaching down, grabbed the other; and that was the way they took him, bumping, jolting, across the road's rutted surface and up the steps to the office. Girt said: "There's a lantern in that closet — light it!" And when Yaggy had done so they stood back and looked him over.

He was not a pretty specimen, laced with the blood of that recent pounding; but he was recognizable and the marshal knew him. So did Girt. "Dave Ruddabaugh!"

"Yeah —" said Yaggy thinly. "One of the Kid's gang. I been waitin' a long time to get my hands on him!"

"You can have him," Girt grunted and, rubbing his lacerated knuckles, took a seat on the edge of the desk. Yaggy got water from the cooler, splashed it on the fellow's face. Presently Ruddabaugh sat up, groaning, blear-eyed. "Well," Yaggy ordered, "start talkin'." And Girt growled: "What was the big idea takin' that shot at me, hombre?"

Ruddabaugh scowled back at them venomously. "You damn fools! It wasn't *me* fired that rifle — I didn't have none! That was *Benson;* an' all I got to say is it's too damn bad he didn't get you!"

"A likely yarn!" Girt scoffed. "What the hell were you doin', then, back of that shack?"

The big outlaw clamped his lips and glared at them. His look said he was all done talking. "That's all right," Yaggy told him. "You're wanted for plenty, bucko.

We'll fat you up for the hangman," he said and, grabbing the owlhooter by the collar, shoved him roughly into a cell.

"You reckon it *was* Cash Benson?" Girt said when Yaggy came back.

The marshal studied the floor cracks thoughtfully; shrugged. "Might of been. What do you figure we better do now?"

"I'm goin' down an' wire Dad Peppin," Girt said grimly. "We need help and we'll get no help in *this* town — they're all friends of Bonney, or scared of him. 'F you think it's safe take the lantern an' see can you unravel them tracks. If it was Benson —"

"Yeah. Might be we could dog his trail."

There was a light in the Express Company's office. With a nod to the fellow on duty Girt picked up a blank and scrawled a message to Peppin. Then, while the agent was sending it, tongue thoughtfully searching cracked lips, Girt laboriously wrote out another:

Sears Roebuck & Comp.
Chicago
   Dear Sears: I ain't wrote you for some time but this is important so oblige by shaking it up some. I want a ring — the

biggest diamond in your factory. Takin' a
whack at double harness, Sears, so keep
your eye on the budget.
> *Yours respeckfully,*
> *Girt Sasabe*
> *Sheriff of Broken Stirrup.*

"You want this sent official?" the agent
asked, looking it over.

"Sure — hell, yes! Charge it to the
county. How long 'fore I'll hear from
Peppin?"

"Three-quarters of an hour, mebbe."

"O.K.," Girt said, and went hurrying
back to the office. Yaggy was brushing his
trousers. "Any luck?" Girt asked.

The marshal nodded; handed him a
button. A large, square, bright blue button;
and Girt's eyes flashed when he saw it.
"Benson's! By grab, I'm through playin'
round with that chipmunk — I'm goin' to
jug him or plant him, one! Can we foller
them tracks?"

"Sure. Pretty near light enough now. Get
your answer from Peppin?"

"Not yet," Girt said, "but I'm goin' back
now an' wait for it. I won't be long, so get
ready to ride — I'm goin' to stop by the
livery an' get me a fresh bronco," he
added; and picking up his Greener that

Yaggy had brought in for him, he shoved a couple of boxes of fresh shells in his pocket and went out.

He kept his eyes skinned as he tramped through the first gray light of a cold false dawn toward Jed Hodgin's stable. He could see his breath plainer than he could see anything else, but he kept a sharp lookout anyhow, not wanting to play target for any more owlhooter sharpshooting. But he reached Hodgins' place without encounter and was a bit surprised to find the stablekeeper awake and at his chores.

There was mud in Hodgins' eye. "Hell of a sheriff *you* are!" he said, and spat contemptuously. "What you reckon I'm payin' taxes for?"

"Damned if *I* know," Girt came back at him. "Tell me."

"I'll tell you all right!" the stable man snarled, raising a fist and shaking it under Girt's nose. "I pay 'em for *protection* an' a lot of protection *you* are!" and he spat again, not missing Girt's boot by a finger. "D'you know I been robbed in the night? Well, I *have!* Some sneakthievin' Judas has lifted the very best nag in my place — that palomino I paid five hundred for las' June!"

Girt looked at him slanchways, set his saddle on the fence and commenced rolling up a smoke. "Hard lines," he mentioned mildly. "Got a match on you anyplace, mister?"

Mechanically Hodgins was reaching toward his hatband when the gall of the sheriff's remark bit home. "Hard lines!" he shouted. "I'll 'hard lines' *you!* That all you can think of to say when a man tells you he's been robbed?"

"Just a minute," Girt cautioned. "I'm thinkin' . . . When'd this happen? Know who it was?"

"You reckon he left me a callin' card!"

"Aw, calm down," Girt growled. "I expect I know who took your bronc an' I'll undertake to get it back if you keep your shirt on a second. 'D he leave his own horse with you?"

"He left a gol darn crowbait that —"

"By grab! Let's see it!"

Dismounting before the Express Office Girt went in and the night man shoved him a paper.

Girt took one squint and went out of the place like a scorpion had crawled up his pantsleg. The message was brief and pungent:

251

You got your chance — go to it

Peppin.

"Well," said Yaggy when Girt reached the office. "I can see you got it — no, never mind showin' it to me; I can tell by your mug what's in it. Guess we might's well shove along; allow it's light enough. You ready?"

Girt nodded, scowling. "By cripes, I'd bust my sides out if we managed to nab the Kid!"

"Yeah — so would I," Yaggy grunted. "But there's no use hopin' for miracles. If we even come up with 'em, it'll be somethin' to tell about. I've sent that pipe off to Santa Fe; we may get somethin' from that."

"Well, I ain't countin' on it," Girt remarked gloomily. "Luck's turned her nose up at me — Oh, by the way! That potshooter was Benson, all right; the nag he rode into Bonney's place on is down at Hodgins' stable. Plumb wore to a frazzle — he took off on Hodgins' palomino."

"Addin' horse-thievin' to the rest of his crimes now, is he? Well, you can always get him for that if the abduction charge won't stick," the marshal said more cheerfully. "Now look —"

252

"Look yourself a minute. I'm anxious as anyone to grab Cash Benson, but seems to me the most important thing right now is to come up with Matheson an' them others. *They're* the ones that's got that bank loot —"

"We don't know that," Yaggy objected; "We only *think* they got it. But anyway, if they got it or not, Benson's the buck to foller."

He swung laboriously into the saddle, abetted by a deal of grunting. Dabbing the sweat from his chins, he heaved a lugubrious sigh, then said: "Now look — here's the way I dope it. Benson, bein' so long a Big Knob around these localities, is bound to be choke-full of pride an' cussedness. That bein' the case, what will he do? Well, he grabbed Matheson's kid to hold her for ransom once — but you an' Bonney put in your oars an' upset the applecart for him. Looks to me like he's bound to have at it again — Now wait!" he said, holding a hand up. "The girl's gone off with Bonney; we don't know where *Matheson's* gone to, but despite havin' the girl along, it's my guess Bonney's joined him — mebbe he figures to use the girl to whip Matheson into line — into a split, if he's got the bank loot. Benson, if he hasn't got the loot, you can bet he has heard about it; that gives him a double incentive — girl plus money. Benson, boy, is goin' to come up with Bonney, Matheson an' company!"

"Fine!" Girt said. "An' we'll come right up back of him —"

"We'll *try*," Yaggy amended dryly.

24

They clung like leeches to Benson's tracks and the tracks brought them into Duran; but they got there half an hour too late. The town was in an uproar — a bedlam fabricated by the clacking curses of the shopkeepers. The place had been robbed! — had been raided! Bonney's gang had swept through like a cyclone and lifted every penny in sight! "Like a bunch of goddam grasshoppers!" one fellow growled in a passion.

Girt said: "Was there a slim young fella in a charro suit with 'em?" and the man glared up at him darkly.

"If you'd been onto your job, by jinks —"

A grinning old coot told Girt with a cackle: "Can't blame Joe, here, fer feelin' a little huffy — three-four of them fellers rode their broncs right into his saloon; an' that there feller you was askin' about shot all Joe's mirrors to splinders an' when Joe up an' ventured a protest, she shot all the bottles off his back bar!"

"She?" Girt said like the term suprised him; and the old man cackled again. "Yeah — eh-heh! 'Twas a *she* all right —"

"Never mind all that!" Yaggy grumbled. "Which way'd they go?"

"You're not allowin' to go after 'em, be you? Jest you two by yourselves? Wal, curl my rudder! You'd ort to be bored fer the simples! If this *town* couldn't stop 'em —"

"Cry-*minie!*" Girt yelled. "Will you hobble your jaw long enough for someone to say which way —"

"Took the road to Vaughn —"

That was all Girt wanted to know. "C'mon!" he muttered at Yaggy, and shook his bronc into a gallop.

"Vaughn's out of your jurisdiction, boy," Yaggy growled when he got up alongside. "You better —"

"Jurisdiction be damned!" Girt snarled. "I'm comin' up with that bunch if I have to chase 'em to Halifax!"

Two miles out from Duran, on the Vaughn road, they struck the palomino's trail again; and suddenly Girt cried excitedly: "By grab! We're playin' this like suckers, Yaggy, follerin' them whippoorwills this way! That ol' fossil back at Duran wasn't half addled at that. Even 'f we come up with them rannies, they're goin' to have all the advantage —"

"I know that," Yaggy grumbled. "But there ain't no way we can git round it —"

"Hell there ain't! We can cut in ahead an' waylay 'em!'

"Swell!" Yaggy said sarcastically. "Ahead of where?"

Girt pulled his horse up in a dust cloud. "They're headin' for the Pecos — bet you anything you wanta name! They're makin' for Pat Coghlin's!"

Yaggy considered, frowning. "Be an awful gamble, boy. If they ain't, them bucks'll git clean away — bank loot, palomino and everything."

"All right; you foller their sign if you want to," Girt said; "I'm short-cuttin' to Coghlin's!" and he raked the black horse with his spurs.

"Told you, by Gawd!" Yaggy said with an oath when, from atop a near hill's overhang, they stared down at Coghlin's ranch buildings. "You guessed wrong, boy — your birds have flown."

It looked, anyway, like *Coghlin* had. The place looked utterly deserted. The corrals were empty and no smoke was rising from the chimney.

Girt said, "We'll go have a look at it

anyhow." Coghlin may have got suspicious about Girt's former visit and bolted — gone back to the Tularosa; but he thought optimistically that was no criterion the Kid and his bunch wouldn't come here. "An' if they don't, we're no worse off by waitin'," he declared grimly. "Time we doubled back an' picked up their sign again, they'd be clean down into Mexico — an' there's always that hideout in the Capitans. We can try that if we don't have no luck any other way."

"Yeah!" Yaggy said pessimistically. "We can try the South Pole, too — but, you can take it from me they won't be there!"

"Aw, go roll a hoop!" Girt snarled, and sent his bronc down the gulchside.

Because of the sharp pitch, the trail he was on angled toward the rear of the place, leading down off the cliff in such manner that it brought him down onto the valley's floor among the clutter of Coghlin's outbuildings. Girt looked back once to see if Yaggy were coming, but the marshal wasn't; he was sitting his horse where Girt left him with the sour look still on his face.

"Hell with him," Girt muttered and reined his horse past the empty blacksmith shop and stables, thinking bitterly how he'd botched the job from first to last. Bonney'd made a monkey of him and so had Benson and Matheson — even Matheson's pants-wearing daughter had played him for a sucker and the whole damn country would laugh at him. "Sasabe?" they would say. "Oh, that tinbadge! Yeah; the Goat of Torrance County's what —"

Girt's imaginings broke off suddenly as his horse took him round the harness shed; and he pulled the black short in its tracks. The back of the house was in plain view now and his heart thumped wildly as he eyed it. A saddled bronc stood on grounded reins beside the door; and there was no imagination about that, by grab!

He slid from the saddle pronto, grabbed his Greener and catfooted forward. He was twenty feet from the door when it opened and the King of Tularosa, minus his black patch and with a bulging sack on his shoulder, came staggering out like he was Atlas packing the world.

Coghlin's jaw dropped; and so did the sack — with a *chunk!* like he'd filled it with lead. "That's fine! Jest stand like that — an' *real steady*," Girt drawled, "unless you want your picture took with this shotgun!"

"Say! What's the big idea?" demanded

Coghlin, glowering; but he kept his hand clear of his gun.

"The idea," Girt grinned maliciously, "is you thought you was pretty dang slick when I went larrupin' out of here yesterday — thought you'd put it all over on me, didn't you? An' if it's any satisfaction, I don't mind sayin' that you did — but I got you with the goods *this* time an', boy, you're goin' up for life!"

"Why you rattleheaded cub! You ain't got nothin' on *me!* Put up that —"

"I'll put a hole through your gizzard they can drive a ten-team hitch through if you don't git them hands up pronto!" Girt snapped as Yaggy larruped up in a lather. "Ain't got nothin' on you, eh? Yaggy —" he told the marshal, "go cut that sack of his open — *Stand still,* you poison spider, or I'll sift you full of daylight!"

Coghlin changed tactics abruptly. "These fierce threats of violence are quite unnecessary, gentlemen." He showed a tolerant smile. "You're not addressing some backwoods outlaw, Sheriff. If you're determined to paw over my belongings —"

"We're goin' to paw all right!"

Smile turned mocking, the King of Tularosa bowed. "Go right ahead; I've nothing to hide. My life and actions are an open book —"

"You must of left out a lot of pages, then! Where's that patch you was sportin' yesterday? Where's all them rifle-toters that was lollin' round the landscape — what were they here for, anyhow, if you're such an aboveboard number? An' why call yourself *Garson* when your —"

"Ah!" Coghlin chuckled. "Now I see! A natural misconception. Yesterday you happened to observe me in a guise I sometimes don for business purposes; today, the need for it having passed, you discover me —"

"Yeah — I've discovered you, all right," Girt told him drily. "Bank lootin's a serious business, hombre, an' you'll be powerfully lucky —"

"*Bank robbery!* What the hell you talkin' about *now?*" demanded the King, an edge of fear and anger tearing through his suavity. "If you're insinuating — why, damn it! I got proof I wasn't anywhere near Broken Stir—"

Girt cried sharply: "Who said anything about Broken Stirrup?"

Coghlin started like a man slapped across the mouth. His high cheeks darkened to a sudden rush of fury.

But Girt grinned coldly. "Figured you'd make a slip if I give you rope enough. Yaggy, lift that business man's pistol, will you?" He chuckled at the baffled anger twisting Coghlin's features. And then to Yaggy: "Cut open that sack an' see if it don't check out to that hundred thousand dollars that's missin' from the bank."

"You mean —" gasped Yaggy, startled, "the bank plunder's in that bag?"

"Damned right! Get busy checkin' it; we're goin' to put this King of Finance away for keeps!"

"But how," Yaggy said, "did you know the loot was in there? Coghlin couldn't hardly have been the bird that took it out of our closet —"

"I didn't know," Girt chuckled; "an' he wasn't. I just guessed it — sort of come to me like a flash when I seen him comin' out the door with all that sacked weight on his shoulder. That sack I put in the closet didn't heft quite the same as when I got it from Matheson. But I didn't think nothin' of it then. One of them birds outside must have switched sacks on me while I was in Coghlin's office dishin' him sauce about Clay Matheson. Reckon he thought he was pretty slick —"

"But, cripes," Yaggy growled. "You'd

look fine tellin' that to a court!" He sighed lugubriously. "We'll never convict him —"

"Hell we won't! We'll just let him do all the talkin' — possession's nine points of the law; he could talk from now till Doomsday without gettin' round his havin' it. We've caught him with the goods an' if he tells the truth we can still send him up. An' Matheson will go right along with him!"

"Well, pick me up, Gerty!" Yaggy cried delightedly, and whacked his thigh at the prospect. "You got a head on your —"

"Shh!" Girt hissed, suddenly stiffening. "Horses — hear 'em? By grab, boy. *They're comin'!*"

From the gloom of the harness shed doorway they could see a moving line of riders; four of them, silhouetted against the copper-stained clouds as they came angling down the rimrock trail in a sweat to get to the house. Coghlin's horse was still outside the back door just as he'd left him and there was nothing, Girt thought, that could possibly warn those approaching horsemen of the trap they were riding into. Their own broncs were in the stable out of sight and from the trail the ranch must have looked as it had a scant hour earlier when Girt had come riding down it.

There was nothing to warn them — nothing. Yet, despite this, something — some sixth sense, perhaps, that is given owlhooters like Bonney — must have warned the Kid in that last moment. They were almost at the stable when, without the slightest preliminary, Bonney whirled his horse on its haunches — sent it lashing up the backtrail.

With an oath Girt dropped his Greener; grabbed for Yaggy's rifle. But the marshal spun away from him. "Don't be a fool! *You want to lose the whole damn bunch?*"

Then Girt was onto him, wrenching the rifle away from him. But when he whirled to fire, Merrilyn Matheson, likewise spurring for the rim, had gotten between him and his target; and muttering wickedly, Girt slammed the gun back at Yaggy, scooped up his Greener and went tearing into the yard.

Benson and Matheson spun in their saddles; Benson's face going darkly bloated as his hand ripped down for his gun.

Girt cried: "Go on, you chipmunk — yank it!" and Matheson reached for the clouds. Benson hung fire, torn between the lust to shoot and fear of that leveled shotgun. At last, with a bitter snarl, he scowlingly raised his hands.

"Keep your gun on 'em," Girt told Yaggy, and jumped forward to get their weapons. Leaning his Greener against the fence, he tore the rifle from Matheson's saddle, took his pistol — tossed both into the brush. "You next!" he gritted, moving toward Benson; and was so riled at the Kid's escape he didn't half read the look on Benson's cheeks. He yanked out the man's rifle, dropped it; took the Colt from Benson's holster and was stepping back, when frantically Yaggy shrilled: *"Look out!"* and immediately flame blossomed from the rustler boss's down-sweeping hand.

Girt lurched, staggered as a white-hot pain bit his shoulder. He had no consciousness of slapping leather, no consciousness of shooting; but through the red fog of his anger he saw Cash Benson reeling from his saddle; heard Yaggy's: "By Gawd, boy! That was *shootin'!*" faintly; then everything went black.

"Where's that Palomino?" Girt grunted, sitting up.

"Hey!" cried Yaggy, excitedly waddling across the room. "Git down there, dang it! You're bad hurt, boy — *you crazy nitwit!* I just got that hole plugged an' there you . . ."

"Never mind that," Girt muttered, bracing a hand against the wall. "How'd I get here? — Coghlin's, ain't it?"

"Sure it's Coghlin's! I carried you in here, that's how; and believe me you was a armful," grumbled Yaggy, flapping around him like an old hen. "Gosh sakes, boy, git off them feet! You wanta start bleedin' all over?"

"I'm all right," Girt insisted. "You got that palomino?"

Yaggy eyed him owlishly. "You must be outa your head, boy! I don't know nothin' about no palo—"

"Hodgins' golden horse that he paid five hundred bucks for . . ."

"Oh — that dang nag! You think I've had time to think about a damfool horse —"

"I promised Hodgins I'd get that prize plug back for him," Girt began; but Yaggy waved him down.

"Well, keep your pants on, boy." The fat man sighed. "He's in the corral an' —" He broke off to curse, exasperated, as a racket broke out in the next room like all the Mescaleros off the reservation were gathered there beating tom-toms. "It's that fool King of Tularosa again!" he glared. "Every time I get set to catch a breath —"

But Girt was in the hall by then and

Yaggy, with a final curse, made after him.

Quite a sight met Girt's narrowed gaze as he pushed the office door open. There, stretched on the floor and tied ankle to ankle and hand to hand, three abreast, with the same piece of rope, were Matheson, Benson and Coghlin. Matheson and Coghlin were drumming their heels, and perforce the dead man drummed, too.

"Cry-*minie!*" Girt said. "I don't wonder they're bellerin', lashed up that way to a stiff. What was the big idea?"

"Just to keep 'em in mind," Yaggy said, "that they might be a lot worse off."

"Well, get that sock out of Coghlin's mouth; he looks like he wants to talk."

Coghlin did, but it took him a while to get going. When he got his jaws working, the King snarled; "You guys think you're pretty slick monkeys pullin' all this tough stuff, but there's a law, by Gawd, in this Territory! You're out of your jurisdiction, an' —"

"You bet on the wrong horse, that time! I'm a U.S. marshal," Yaggy told him, "an' the sheriff here is my deputy — all legal as a law book," and Girt tipped his hat derisively.

Back in the living room Yaggy said: "Well, I got that bank loot checked and sacked an' the plunder they lifted from Duran — most of it anyways; the Kid got away with a little. The palomino's safe-tied in the corral an' — shucks, boy, don't take it so to heart. That chessycat's cut loose of better guys than us — set the whole durn Territory on its ear and made an ape of Axtell, to boot! You've done dang well-good as *anyone* could. We've got the swag an' three of the guys, not countin' Ruddabaugh or that teller. What if the Kid *did* get away? As fer that pants-wearin' female —"

"Hell, I ain't worryin' about *her!*"

Yaggy eyed him dubiously. "No," he said finally, "I guess not . . . What you figurin' to do with the reward fer that Flyer loot, if you get it? Fer that stuff that was in the Kid's pipe?"

"How much reward they offering?"

"Close on to five thousand dollars."

"Cry-*minie!*" Girt swore. "Reckon I'll buy into the cow business if I got that much c—" He broke off suddenly to stare through the open window. *"D'rinthy!"* he cried joyously; and then she was there in the room.

"What've *you* come traipsin' over here for?" demanded Yaggy, scowling.

"For that fool Tinbadge — that's what!

Look at him! All shot up," she wailed. "I just *knew* he couldn't take care of himself!"

And Girt grinned happily, recollecting his wire to Roebuck.

We hope you have enjoyed this Large Print book. Other Thorndike Press or Chivers Press Large Print books are available at your library or directly from the publishers.

For more information about current and upcoming titles, please call or write, without obligation, to:

Thorndike Press
295 Kennedy Memorial Drive
Waterville, ME 04901
Tel. (800) 223-1244

OR

Chivers Press Limited
Windsor Bridge Road
Bath BA2 3AX
England
Tel. (0225) 335336

All our Large Print titles are designed for easy reading, and all our books are made to last.